Winter

NEVERLAND

AN ANTHOLOGY

I0738829

Sam Baker | Krystle Kwiatkowski

Paul E. Petty | J Douglas Burton

Brittany Evans | Chelsea Lauren

IF
Books

Winter NEVERLAND

AN ANTHOLOGY

Sam Baker

Paul E Petty

Brittany Evans

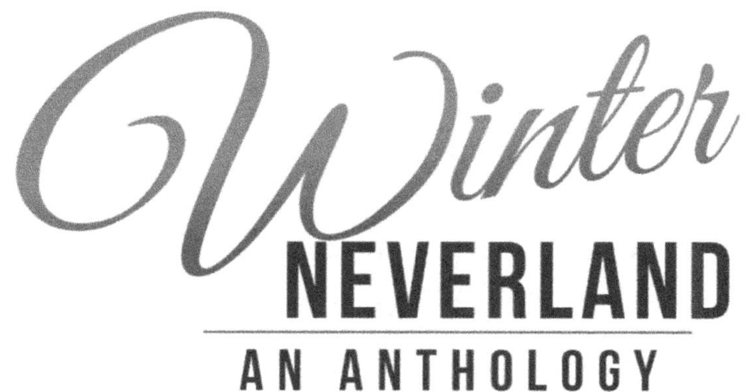

Copyright © 2017 by If Books Publishing

Copyright of individual works belong to their respective authors.

Title page snowflake art by Brittany Evans

Front cover design by J Douglas Burton

Back cover design by Sam Baker

Printed in the United States of America

First If Books Publishing paperback edition 2017

10 9 8 7 6 5 4 3 2 1

ISBN 978-0-9992036-2-0 (print)

ISBN 978-0-9992036-3-7 (ebook)

Dedicated to each other

because we couldn't have done it alone.

Table of Contents

Tomorrow | *Sam Baker*

Yesterday, today, tomorrow.
Rinse and repeat … and repeat … and repeat.

This can't be right.
How many times have I gone to bed
and thought it was Christmas Night?

But I didn't just think … I knew.
I knew from the gift wrap—
red and blue.

I knew from the candy canes,
tall mugs of hot chocolate,
heavy frozen rain.

Yesterday, today, tomorrow.
What happens after this?
How long will I play in the snow,
soak in the holiday bliss?

Yesterday, today, tomorrow.
There's just one thing I must know.
Will there ever be an end
to this forever Christmas land?

It was Brian's 342nd Christmas in a row.

Less than a year since he had moved to town to be closer to his grandparents. And already he couldn't imagine himself living anywhere else.

No, literally: he couldn't imagine it. Whenever Brian attempted to cast his mind back to life before this town, the memories got… a little hazy.

Dr Jefferson said there was nothing to worry about; it was just a standard part of the adjustment from moving to a new place. And if anyone knew what they were talking about, it would obviously be the best doctor in town!

Also the only doctor in town. It was a small town, and no one ever *really* seemed to get sick.

Imagine being sick on Christmas! Horrible.

Sitting at the table, about to tuck into his grandma's Christmas dinner, Brian looked back at the pile of goodies he'd got off his grandparents this morning. Despite the fact that he was now 22 years old, Nan and Gramps spoiled him like he was still a little tyke. He loved them so much for it.

Not that he had skimped on the 'giving' part of the deal; oh no! Being able to make the lives of those he loved just that little bit better, no matter his meagre funds? Terrific!

He never held back when it came to giving, and both his grandparents seemed very happy with what he had brought for them this Christmas.

"Oh no, Nan." As the old lady brought out a turkey the size of the Isle of Wight, Brian objected in appreciative concern. "This is too much. Bloody hell, I'm still full up from yesterday's Christmas dinner."

"Now, now," she chided, grinning as she sat down at the head of the table. "Nothing's too good for my sweet Brian." Turning her wrinkled face toward her husband, she said, "Harold, be a dear and carve the turkey, would you?"

"By 'eck, Greta, you've gone and roasted a monster." Gramps tugged at his stripey jumper as he heaved his bulk to a stand with a puff of air from his moustachioed mouth. "Am I meant to carve this beast or slay it with a lance?"

She swatted him playfully on the arm, and Gramps slipped Brian a private wink. With all the other food already laid out on the table, there was no way the three of them could polish off this prehistoric-sized bird.

There'd be plenty of leftovers for tomorrow's Christmas dinner, that's for damn sure.

As he laid three thick slices of meat on Brain's plate, Gramps asked him, "You're takin' some of this home wi' you, right lad?"

What could he do but agree?

✳✳✳

Brain struggled to close the door of his car, laden as he was with bags full of presents and several plastic containers worth of leftovers Nan and Gramps had insisted on sending him home with.

As if he would have room in his swollen belly for any of that food tonight—or tomorrow, what with the equally lavish spread Nan was sure to set out for Christmas dinner again.

Eventually he succeeded in closing and locking the car;

the next trick was to somehow get inside his house without dropping any of these treasures. Fiddling with the keys, Brian hoisted some of his burden up in front of his face to clear room for his hand to fumble its way to the lock.

How he managed it without spilling any of his goodies Brian would never know, but he soon stomped inside the front door, shaking the caked snow off his trainers. With a sigh, he dumped the bags off onto the floor and hauled the food away to the fridge.

In between the containers of food from the last few Christmases, there was *just enough* room to slide these ones. Brian wondered when he'd have time to polish off these lovely leftovers, what with a new Christmas dinner every day. He hoped they wouldn't go to waste.

Now picking back up the bags again that he had left by the door, he began the search for a place to store these new presents.

Easier said than done.

"Blimey." Each door he opened in his semi-detached home was stuffed to the brim with previous gifts. A mountain of them toppled onto Brian on one occasion, and he spent the next forty-five minutes just putting them back as he had found them.

He hoped none of the electronics had been broken.

"So where the bloody hell am I gonna put these?"

Sure, it was a great problem to have—so many nice things that there was literally nowhere to store them—but it *was* still a problem. He'd gone into every cupboard, every spare living space, and found no area unoccupied by… something.

Except… what was that? There, at the end of the hall.

Brian didn't remember that door being there. Funny the things you let slip past your attention, innit?

The door opened with a creak, and he was delighted to find that an entire storage room that he had never known existed was right here in this hallway the whole time!

"Right under me nose," he mumbled to himself. "It's a funny old world, eh?"

***

Christmas morning dawned, and Brian awoke with the same eager excitement he had felt since he was a child. Back then, of course, Christmas had only come *once* a year; he could only *imagine* the enthusiasm he would have felt as child experiencing so many of them in a row.

Despite the chilly temperature, as soon as he'd had his shower and mug of coffee, Brian felt the need to go for a walk outside. Burn off a few of the five million calories he'd taken in yesterday—just in time to eat his own weight in turkey again today!

As he strolled along the picturesque streets of the town, Brian thought back once again to the oddity of discovering that storage room in his house for the first time last night. He must be a right blind bastard never to have seen that before.

He supposed you just got used to only looking for the things you expected to find. That must be it.

Approaching Main Street, he caught sight of Mr Spencer outside his little shop, using a broom taller than himself to reach the sill atop his sign and brush the foot or so of snow off of it. The windows of the shop were barred by a metal grille, and a notice with illustrations of holly proclaimed that the establishment was "Closed for Christmas".

"Oy, Mr Spencer!" Brian waved a gloved hand at the shopkeeper, removing it from his pocket just long enough to greet the man before replacing it and huffing more cold air into his pained lungs.

Stupid cold day to take a walk, he cursed himself as he went.

"Hey, Brian lad!" The man's bulbous nose was red with veins and his cheeks looked like someone had stuck two flesh-coloured golf balls to the side of his face as he grinned. "How's the grandparents?"

"Good, good." He came to a stop in front of Mr Spencer, half-burying his face in his coat for warmth. "Driving over there in a minute for dinner."

"My wife's got our turkey in the oven right now," the man proclaimed jovially. "Just getting the shop here cleaned off, ready for business."

Something struck Brian as being odd just now, but he couldn't quite put his finger on it.

"You're… not open today, surely?"

Mr Spencer laughed easily. "Lawks no, lad. It's Christmas, innit?"

Brian nodded sagely, still frowning to himself. "So… you're getting ready for tomorrow?"

The smile fell from Mr Spencer's face as he failed to comprehend what Brian was getting at. "Eh? Course not. Still be Christmas, won't it?"

He was right; of course he was right. But if Mr Spencer wasn't getting the place ready for today, or tomorrow…

"So," Brian began, feeling out the gist of what he wanted to know as he spoke, "if you're not open—and nobody is—when will you be?"

The man shook his head, his grey hair flying wild in a sudden gust of bitter wind. "Not on Christmas, that's for damn sure. You all right, Bri?"

"Yeah. Fine." Something didn't make sense here. "So where'd I buy my presents?"

"Eh?"

"The presents." He was starting to grasp the edges of what felt wrong. "The ones I'm giving out. Where'd I get 'em?"

"Not here." Mr Spencer shrugged, casual but clearly starting to worry about his conversation partner. "Mebbe from Mrs Goldsmith's place down the street."

"Nah." Brian shook his head firmly. "Closed an' all, in't she? So where'd I buy them?"

Mr Spencer didn't even seem to understand the question—never mind have an answer ready—but Brian kept going, gaining speed as he went, comprehension building like a snowball racing down a hill.

"And where'd Nan and Gramps get theirs? Come to that, where'd any of us get the money to buy the bloody things? Not working, are we, what with the holidays an' all."

Patting Brian patronisingly on the shoulder, Mr Spencer said softly, "Get back home, lad. I think the cold's messing with yer 'ead."

Realising he would get nowhere with this man, Brian smiled back, seeing the cloud of steam rise up from his nostrils as he puffed a response.

"Probably right. See ya, Mr Spencer."

The shopkeeper waved good-bye, but nursed a private look of concerned bafflement as he turned back to his home a few doors down.

None of this had ever occurred to Brian before—and that was as concerning to him as the questions themselves.

Christmas. Every day. Wizzard would have *loved* this place.

Where did everyone buy the bloody presents? And when? And how?

And then there was the storage space. Brian had run out of room in his house, when suddenly there was a whole extra room he'd never sodding noticed before. It didn't make sense.

None of it made sense. Just what the bloody hell was going on in this town?

That's when he noticed the bearded man in the anorak, standing on the street corner.

Just watching him.

The intensity of the bloke's stare was unnerving, but he didn't seem particularly up to anything. Not creepy as such. Just… standing.

Staring.

"You all right, mate?" Brian shouted to the man. He didn't reply.

Curious, but cautious, Brian started forwards in the man's direction. The bloke didn't flinch, but neither did he relax or change his behaviour. Just continued to stand stock-still, dark eyes examining Brian analytically.

As soon as he was a few feet from the fellow, Brian came

to a stop, looking the man over in the same searching way he was being stared at.

An ordinary guy, as far as could be told from a cursory examination. Shoes a bit worn, anorak old but in good nick, a bobbled stocking cap pulled tight over his somewhat greasy hair. Behind the beard, he was probably a decent-enough-looking chap, even if that scowl looked enough to drive off any woman who might be interested.

"You got a problem there?"

And then at last the man spoke, his voice rich and lilting (Brian thought there might be a hint of a Welsh accent in there, but he couldn't be sure):

"No problem. Just… couldn't help overhearing."

Unconsciously, Brian looked back over his shoulder at the spot under Mr Spencer's sign where he had just had that enlightening discussion.

"What, that? Was nothing, mate. Just a bit of banter, was all."

Finally a hint of a smile touched the other man's face. "You're beginning to see. Beginning to see the truth."

Brian frowned. "What truth?"

"The truth about this town."

What Brian hated most was how crazy the man sounded, when he was talking about the *exact* same thing Brian just had been.

Is that what Mr Spencer heard? he thought to himself. Me sounding like a prat with a conspiracy theory? No wonder he buggered off in such a hurry. Maybe all of that shit I was thinking about was nothing after all.

Maybe I should just forget all about it.

"There's nothing wrong with this town," he insisted to the stranger, hunching his shoulders against the ill wind.

"You know there is." The man seemed unaffected by the howling gusts; the anorak he wore didn't look all *that* warm. "There's a secret here. A dark one. You've just come to the very edges of it, Brian."

That startled him. "How… How do you know my name?"

The bloke lifted his bearded chin in the direction of the shop. "The fellow you were talking to said it."

Oh. Well that was all right, then.

"You have to follow the clues, Brian. You have all the cards; it's just a matter of playing them in the right order."

Cards? Eh? Brian wasn't following this analogy.

"Yer wot, mate?"

Narrowing his eyes, the beardy bloke brought one hand out of his pocket and reached towards Brian.

"Here," he said firmly. "Take it."

In the chap's calloused hands was a strange piece of metal, like an old medallion. Mostly round, in an intricate if indecipherable, design. One segment of the carved centre curved outwards like a coat hook.

Brain felt like he was being offered pirate treasure.

"What is it?"

No answer was given in response. Just that single, steady hand proffered in assurance.

With a sigh, Brian took the odd piece of metal from the stranger, pocketing it quickly.

Relief spread across the man's face then, and he took a half-step backwards with a smile.

"One more question before I leave, Brian."

"Okay." He frowned again, still unsure what the point of this encounter was.

"The town. The one we're in. What's its name?"

"Eh?" What a stupid question. "It's…"

Huh. That *was* weird. All of a sudden, Brian had no idea what the name of this bloody town was!

But that didn't make sense. He'd lived here for nearly a year, after all. And anyway, it had to be listed on some of the shops and whatnot, didn't it?

"Town Market". "Town Centre Square". "Best Chips in Town".

Town, town, town. Nothing with an actual name on it!

It had to have a name, though. Brian would have noticed if he lived some place that didn't even have a bloody name!

Just like he would have noticed that extra room in his house?

"You see it, don't you?" The bearded man smiled, taking an extra step back. "You see now. This has been an excellent talk, Brian. I'm so glad we had it before I needed to go."

Go? Go whe--

Brian reached out in panic at the man backing up right onto the white street—just as a snowplough sped around the corner.

A sigh of relief escaped the stranger's lips as the vehicle ran him over, never seeing him even as it rode through his fallen body.

As the plough passed by, all that remained of the man was a trail of red snow left behind the vehicle.

Brian felt like he was going to be sick.

***

Slamming the door behind him, Brian ran to the toilet, kneeling by it in case he heaved. After a few minutes of careful breathing, it became clear that he was not going to spew—a fact for which he was truly grateful.

It had been a while since he'd had to experience such nastiness, even with all the Christmas cheer he pounded down most nights. The scene he had just witnessed had been horrific, but there was no need to compound that with the unpleasantness of chucking his bloody guts out, now was there?

That was when the letterbox chapped.

Was someone at the door? It wasn't the kind of loud pounding people used to get your attention; rather Brian had heard the soft, subtle sound of the post being delivered.

But there wouldn't be any post. It was Christmas. No one delivered post on Christmas Day!

Getting up, Brian wound his way around the corner to get a look at the front door. Sure enough, there on the welcome mat was a piece of mail.

A card. A Christmas card.

Who would be sending Brian a Christmas card? 342 Christmases in a row, he had received nothing of the sort. So why now?

Unreasonably nervous, he reached out ever so slowly for the envelope. Grabbed onto it.

Waited.

No surprises. No shocks, or explosions.

It was just a Christmas card.

Laughing, and with a rueful shake of his head, Brian looked at the front of the envelope. Sure enough, there was his name and address. Postmarked today: Christmas.

So who delivered it?

And the writing: no handwriting that he recognised. Scrawled in dark blue ink with a hand apparently unused to trying to convey readable information to anyone else, it was completely foreign to Brian.

What the hell? he figured. May as well open it.

After slitting along the top with his finger, Brian gingerly removed the card from its casing. The front was a bland cartoon of a reindeer in the snow. No text.

Inside was no personalised message, or even the usual preprinted platitudes. Only a number, written in large bold characters:

13

"Huh." Scowling, he tilted the card this way and that, attempting to spot some hidden message or other. There was nothing. "Unlucky for some, I suppose."

"You can say that again."

Brian dropped the card in fright, turning on the spot to try and see the source of the intruder's voice. There was no sign of anyone in the vicinity, but the words had seemed to come from right next to him.

"Hello?" he called out, voice trembling. Slowly, he took two cautious steps toward his living room.

Who had invaded Brian's home without him noticing? What were they doing here, on Christmas Day of all times?

Maybe they were after the enormous hoard of gifts he

had received over the last 342 days; it was possible.

Clearing his throat, Brian tried again: "Is anyone there?"

"Oh, for goodness' sake." The voice was low, thick, and somewhat muffled—seeming to come now from somewhere behind him.

Back towards the front door.

There was no one there. No one Brian could see anyway.

"Who are you?" He swallowed, inching closer to the door. "Where are you?"

"For god's sake, I'm right where you bloody dropped me!"

Odd. It was almost as if…

The sound was coming from the Christmas card. But of course it was.

With great trepidation, Brian bent to pick the card up from the ground, and looked at the front of it again.

This time the cartoon reindeer on the front had an expression of extreme annoyance on its face, the huge nostrils flared even further to become two gaping holes in its enormous face.

"Whachoo have to go and do that for anyway?"

The reindeer was talking to him.

Again: the illustrated reindeer on the front of the mysterious Christmas card was moving its giant lips and actually talking to Brian!

"Um, what?" It was the best he could manage at that moment.

"You dropped me." The reindeer's tone was indignant. "Fell right on me antlers. Going to have a right pain in them all night now, thank you ever so."

Having never accidentally injured a cartoon character before, he wasn't at all sure what to say.

"Er. Sorry?"

The reindeer dipped its antlers and huffed a gravelly snort. "All right then. So we going or what?"

"Excuse me?"

He knew he sounded dense as all buggery, but Brian really did not have a Scooby what was going on here at all. Perhaps seeing that man get killed on the street had triggered a psychotic break?

But no. The paranoia had begun before that. When he realised the absurdity of this town, that it was always Christmas, and no one ever worked to earn the money they spent on the festivities.

"We've got the next card to pick up ain't we?" The reindeer sounded like he was talking to a five-year-old. "Can't get to where you're going without all three clues, can ya?"

Before Brian could question the Christmas card on what exactly it was talking about (and wasn't *that* a strange thing to have to say!) the telephone in the other room rang.

"I--"

It rang again.

With a sigh, Brian gripped the card tightly in his hand ("Oi!" the card complained) and went through to answer it.

"Hello?"

"Brian love." It was Nan. "Gramps and I weren't sure you were okay. You still coming over for tea?"

Staring at the impatient reindeer on the front of his card, Brian reluctantly replied, "I'll be over in a bit. Something came up. Keep dinner warm for me, won't you?"

"Of course we will, sweetheart. See you when you come over."

"Bye."

"Bye!"

No sooner had the receiver been put back on the hook than the reindeer spoke up once more.

"Get a move on, then. We've only got till the end of the night to do this thing."

What had he got himself into?

***

A slight flurry had begun, the stiff breeze blowing a cloud of powdery snowflakes right into Brian's red face as he walked along Caldwell Avenue with his hands in his pockets. The Christmas card made several muffled noises of complaint from its crumpled position in one of those pockets, but Brian's hand had been too freezing to keep it out—even with gloves on.

Once in a while he spotted someone else on the street and waved jovially hello, but by and large he was alone in his strange journey. Which was all well and good.

The card had told him to go down this street—which is the most bizarre statement Brian could imagine himself ever making.

And then… what?

"Okay, Rudolph," he said with a sigh, taking the card from his pocket and looking at the reindeer painted on it. "Now what?"

"First of all," the cartoon character replied grumpily, "I'm not Rudolph, I'm Dasher."

"Sorry."

"And I'm not really him either. Just a cartoon of him."

Brain paused in his tracks for a moment. "You mean there's a *real* Dasher?"

"I don't--" The reindeer sighed, lifting one hoof in exasperation to its painted face. "How am I supposed to know that? I'm a bloody greeting card. Just… do what I tell you to, eh?"

Snippily, Brian asked, "And what's that, exactly?"

"You know the song *Highway to Hell?*"

"Er, no."

The card looked bemused. "Okay, forget that then. But you know what a road is, yeah?"

"Of course."

"Go down it then."

Brian was not entertained by this exchange. "I already am, thanks. Then what?"

"Turn left. You're looking for Santa's Grotto."

"You have got to be shitting me."

"I don't shit, Brian. I'm a cartoon, remember?"

He supposed there was some logic to that statement. After a fashion.

Santa's Grotto, though? The place in the town centre where kids sat on some guy's lap while he wore a fake white beard and didn't even grumble when they peed all over his red suit?

That Santa's Grotto?

Still, as weird as this day was getting, nothing would surprise him any more.

It didn't take him long to approach the shopping

district—with all the shops closed, of course. In the square, a gaudily-decorated hut surrounded by cotton wool snow bore a sign announcing to all that the grotto was closed for the season.

Santa, after all, would be busy delivering presents by now, wouldn't he? Couldn't sit here letting little tykes piss all down his leg when he had work to do.

"This is the place." Dasher sounded smug in his pronouncement.

"All right then," Brian sighed. "Now what?"

"Go inside the grotto."

Squinting at the grimy plastic hut which had clearly not been designed to accept actual human occupants, Brian asked, "In there? You sure?"

"Positive."

And so he began his trek across the fake snow, just as it began to be covered with a light dusting of the real stuff. Dotted all over the place were brightly-coloured decorations of various types, and he was careful not to stand on any of them.

"Oh!" Dasher's voice was abrupt and filled with alarm. "Watch out for the--"

"Argh!"

Brian looked down to see what had cut into his leg. In shock, he saw that something bright red and white striped had opened its toothy mouth and clamped down onto the flesh of his shin.

"--candy canes!"

"Bloody hell!"

Sure enough, from all over the kitschy display chittering

candy canes began popping up, hopping stiffly but rapidly in his direction.

The one currently latched onto his leg had needle-like teeth which were already beginning to draw blood. The red drops on the snow fit right in with the rest of the decor.

"I'll be buggered!" he cried, shaking his leg in half-fear, half-pain, half-amusement.

Yeah, that was three halves; Brian never had been much cop at maths.

Within moments, more of the little creatures were on him, leaping at his body, teeth sinking into any patch of exposed skin. He stumbled backwards, feet slipping in snow both real and false, flailing each limb independently.

He screamed then, overwhelmed and in shock at such a surprising and frankly painful development.

"Don't scream, Brian." It was the Christmas card talking, lying in the snow where he had dropped it when one of the candy canes munched on his little finger. "They feed on your fear."

"They're feeding on my blimmin' flesh!"

Two more candy canes revealed their needle-like teeth and sank them into his skin. Brian yelped one more time, brushing three of the hook-shaped monsters off his leg as five more approached.

"You have to show 'em who's boss!" Dasher's voice sounded insistent, though it was slowly being muffled by the snow kicked up around and onto the card.

Shaking his arm violently and slapping at the critters covering him, Brain squealed in desperation: "What the hell does that mean?"

"Bite them back, Brian!"

In some strange way, the advice made sense. Biting candy canes was the natural order of things after all, and not the other way around.

Leaning down to where one of the beings was attached to his shoulder by its teeth, Brain opened wide and chomped down.

The candy cane's button eyes widened in fear and pain as Brian tasted the peppermint sweetness of its crunchy flesh. A horrifying shriek arose from its tiny maw as it yielded, releasing Brian from its myriad pointed teeth.

Flakes of white and red crumbled and spilled on the ground as the candy cane fell. Once it hit the snow it tumbled off as fast as its awkward form could take it, mewling all the way.

Emboldened, Brian bared his teeth and snapped at another of the candy canes on him, but as it happened that was all it took.

The creatures all let go of him at once, retreating in fear. Where they went to he could not tell, but the army of tiny beings vanished as quickly as they had appeared.

Whistling in disbelief, Brian advanced on the Christmas card he had dropped before picking it up and dusting it off.

"Quick thinking, mate," he greeted with genuine pleasure. "Ta for that."

"No problem," the card replied. "Now get into that Grotto before something else comes up to get at you."

"Something else?" He didn't want to know about that.

Ducking low, Brian squeezed his bulk into the tiny plastic hut that served as Santa's Grotto for the shopping centre.

It was, of course, mere decoration and not designed to be actually entered into. On the inside of the plastic molded windowsill, however, Brian saw a second envelope sitting there.

His for the taking.

"Go on then," Dasher urged.

Putting that card into his pocket, Brian reached out and removed the next one from its sheath. On the front was what looked like an oil painting of a blue Christmas bauble hanging from a tree branch. Inside was the single word:

Well

Printed in a sans-serif font, bold as you please.

"What on earth is that supposed to mean?"

"That's for you to find out, I suppose."

He shouldn't have been, but Brian was startled enough by the new voice to practically drop the card in response. Shaking his head at his own ridiculousness, he closed the card and looked at the painted bauble.

Sure enough, there on the blue ornament were two large cartoon eyes and a crescent mouth smiling maniacally at him.

"So you're one of them as well, eh? Another chatterbox Chrimbo card?"

"Fraid so, mate." Its voice was chipper and high-pitched, like one of those chipmunks in the old cartoons.

"And you don't know what the word inside you means?"

"What I know and what I can say are not necessarily the same thing, me old china."

Weary of these games, Brian replied, "Does that mean you don't know, or what?"

"It means," the bauble explained patiently, "that you should get going before it's too dark."

"Dark? Why?"

"The old forest gets mighty creepy after nightfall."

Old forest. Creepy.

But of course.

***

"Where are we going again?"

It seemed like the 92nd time Brian had asked that.

"That's the twenty-third time you've asked that," the Christmas card complained. "Just keep following the road, and I'll address the issue when we get there."

"Bob," Dasher warned the bauble in a stern voice. "You're getting a little close to… you know."

"Well who are *they* to tell us what we can and can't say," Bob complained.

Meanwhile, Brian was getting very lost.

"Eh?"

"Never you mind," Dasher said firmly. His card was underneath Bob's, both held in Brian's gloved hand as he strode down the darkening street, hunched over for warmth.

"I swear, I have no idea what's going on any more."

Bob the bauble replied cagily, "Well, each idea has a home, Brian. You just need to find it."

"That's enough, Bob!" Dasher snapped.

Bob blew a raspberry in response.

They continued in silence then for a few more minutes before one of the cards yelled: "Stop! Turn here!"

There was no new road here. Just a bent-down fence

leading into…

Oh. A dark forest. That's right.

"You, er, want me to go into these woods. In the dark. Alone?"

It was only dusky outside, but with the snowfall and the densely-packed trees, the forest was in a blanket of heavy darkness. Brian did *not* like the look of it at all.

"You're not alone at all, my friend!" Bob countered. "We're with you."

What a comfort, he sighed internally. And stepped over the beaten-down fence to enter the creepy woods.

Immediately he wished he'd brought a torch on this little adventure—but he hadn't expected to be out so late, never mind skulking around in a spooky forest. Grabbing an electric light wasn't exactly priority number one when you went out following instructions from a talking Christmas card.

God, Brian's life had got weird recently.

He could barely see a thing among these trees, except hulking shadows a few shades darker than the general near-black all around him. A scuffling sound came to him then from his immediate left, and Brian froze in panic.

"You guys hear that?" he whispered.

"Uh." One of the Christmas cards cleared its nonexistent throat. "Nope. Nothing. Why don't you, er, pick up the pace a little there, Brian, eh?"

Not bad advice.

Jerking his head right and left at every innocent sound he heard around him, Brian did his level best to stick to the barely-trodden path beneath his feet. While craning his neck at one particularly loud rumble, though, he found himself slamming into a large tree directly in his path.

"Oof. Sorry." He'd just apologized to a tree.

Laughing at his own stupidity, Brian shook his head and stepped around the massive trunk.

But somehow it was in his way again.

"That's funny." The path below seemed to run right underneath the massive pine tree. How on earth did that happen?

So Brian strafed left and made another attempt to get round the tree.

And there it was again—right in his way.

Was it just a lot bigger than he had first anticipated? No, no, Brian could quite clearly see the edges of the trunk. Wider than his own body, but easy to step around.

So why couldn't he seem to manage it?

Okay: different tack. Brian turned ninety degrees to the right and made to step forward, but a different tree now hemmed him in.

This one was deciduous, branches bare as a babe in the bathtub. And it pressed right up against the pine tree in Brian's way, cutting off that avenue of escape.

"Uh, guys," he said slowly to the Christmas cards in his hand. "This is getting a little strange."

"Yeah," Bob the bauble piped up regretfully. "We were sort of hoping this wouldn't come up, but…"

"Lemme guess." Brian sighed. "The trees in this wood are alive."

"Just a bit."

"Awesome."

Something scraped against Brian's back and he screamed a high C. Swivelling on the spot, he saw the branches of a third tree pawing at him, encompassing him in their twiggy tendrils.

He couldn't quite catch any of the trees in the act of moving, but somehow, they were—right in front of him. But in the darkness, he couldn't make out the details.

A second pine tree formed a fourth wall, hemming Brian in entirely.

"We're trapped!" he yelped.

Dasher brayed—in terror or in anger, Brian couldn't quite tell. "Do something you moron. Can't you, like, climb one of them or something?"

"I never was any good at climbing trees," he admitted, adrenaline pumping something awful. As one of the trees continued to manhandle him, another pressed in tight as though ready to make him the meat in a wood sandwich.

In desperation, Brian attempted to clamber up the handsy tree in front of him, but the branches moved out of his way, causing him to do little more than add a series of abrasions to the teeth-marks already covering his skin beneath shredded trouser-legs.

He was a goner this time, for sure. But then:

"Hey, you guys smell that?"

Something other than the mulchy smell of the forest drifted over on the breeze. It was smoke, but not the cigarette kind he craved for this first time now in he couldn't remember how long.

No, it was something else; something richer.

"A log fire!"

The Christmas cards made sniffing noises, though Brian didn't think that they had real noses to sample the air.

"You're right!" Dasher declared in delight. "It's a fire!"

"A real one," Bob sighed in relief.

At first, Brian wasn't at all certain why the cards were so pleased at this turn of events. But a creaking sound arose from the trees, one that resembled nothing so much as a groan of fear: and suddenly Brian found his path clear.

The trees which had enclosed him, pressing in, scraping at his flesh, were suddenly gone altogether. No sight of them. And, in fact, a wide swath cut through the woods to the exit not far from where he stood.

Straight to a rustic little cabin with smoke belching forth from the chimney.

"I guess that's where the fire is," he observed.

"And why don't you get to it, lickety-split?" Dasher advised, and Brian took his point immediately.

The trees had been scared off by the smell of fire, but once they understood it to be contained they would not hesitate to attack Brian again. So he'd best scarper before that happened.

In a jiffy, he found himself swinging open the cabin's door with a loud creak and running inside to safety.

The building consisted of just one moderate-sized room, simply decorated but pleasing and homey. A roaring fire burned in the fireplace, one rocking chair swayed back and forth lightly as though but recently vacated, and on a small table next to the seat was an envelope.

And the remains of a Christmas card.

"What's going on?" Bob shrieked in despair as they got

close enough to see the scene before them.

No one was here in the cabin but Brian and the cards, so who had lit the fire? And who had done… this?

On the table was the front half of the third Christmas card—torn unevenly in two. Adorning the card was a poorly-sketched elf, but his torso had been bifurcated by the tear, and pencil-lined blood pooled on the page behind him.

The eyes of the illustrated elf were mercifully closed, but it was obvious the character was dead.

"Fuck me," Dasher bleated.

Over in the fireplace, Brain could see the remains of the rear portion of the card, ripped into even smaller pieces and burnt now mostly to ashes.

Whatever clue the card had contained was lost now to the ages.

"Someone got to Jim," Bob declared. "They could get to us next!"

"Not likely," Dasher disagreed, and leapt from Brian's hand.

Bob was close behind him, and together the two cards flapped their pages like wings and soared out through the front door of the cabin. Up, up and away, never to be seen again.

Distraught, Brian held onto the door jamb, watching the strange creatures fly out of sight. "But what am I supposed to do now?"

If they answered him, he never heard it.

In desperation, Brian ran to the fireplace, grabbing at a few charred fragments of card at the edge of the glowing logs. The skin on his fingers singed, but no great damage was done—which was more than could be said for the remains of the Christmas card.

Whatever message had been written inside was long since gone. From the scraps he had before him, Brian figured that there may have been a "t"—and definitely an "n"—but those small clues did him little good.

All of this adventuring—the bite marks he still bore from baby killer candy canes, the scratches from deadly moving trees—led only to this. To a fruitless collection of burnt scraps and his memories of what was printed inside the other two cards.

"13".

"Well".

Just what was that supposed to mean? And who had broken in here ahead of Brian to get rid of the evidence?

Come to think of it, who provided the evidence in the first place? He had somehow associated all of this with the weird bearded guy who turned himself into plough-jam, but that bloke had had no opportunity to post the first card between seeing Brian's conversation with Mr Spencer and his death shortly thereafter.

Apparently someone was monitoring the goings-on in this town. Perhaps more than one person; both opposed to the status quo, and in favour of it.

So was it all for naught? Was this the end of Brian's journey? Here, in an empty (but quite toasty thanks to the roaring fire) cabin at the far end of the forest bordering his small town?

Maybe there was some way to piece together the clues he'd already been given. The number 13. The word "well".

What could they mean together?

Thirteen was an unlucky number, so you wouldn't be well if you came across it? But what would that have to do with *any*thing?

And that still didn't help him with the missing third word. Something with a "t" and an "n".

Sitting on a rug by the fire, Brian toyed with the scraps in front of him. Had the other two cards known more about the situation than they had let on? Did they know what was written inside them, what the clues meant?

He had a good feeling they did. After all, Dasher had warned Bob against spilling the beans when the latter appeared to be trying to tell Brian a little too much.

But wait: what *had* he said?

Brian racked his brains, trying to recall. They'd been walking along the street and then… what?

Eventually the phrase came to his mind, but it meant little more now than it had at the time.

"Just keep following the road, and I'll address the issue when we get there."

Well, Brian *had* followed the road, and it had led here. What was it that Dasher found so objectionable in that statement?

Hang on, though, wasn't there something else? Yeah, that's right, the card had also been told off for following it up with:

"Well, each idea has a home, Brian. You just need to find it."

Road. Address. Home.

Could it be…?

Now that Brian thought about it, one of the first things that Dasher had said to him was to ask if he knew the song *Highway to Hell.*

Another road reference—though given Dasher's wariness, that one may have simply slipped out subconsciously.

It all added up, though. The number, the words.

They were a street address.

***

Brian was back in town now, and darkness had fallen utterly. The snow had stopped, but a nice thin sheet of it crunched noisily under his feet—as much like ice particles as it was powdery fluff.

Despite the cold, a sheen of sweat coated his forehead. He was power-walking, determined to make it to his destination as quickly as possible.

13 Wellington Road.

He was sure that was the answer to the riddle. No other street in town began with "well"—certainly not with a "t" or an "n" in the rest of its name.

That had to be the end of the line for this quest. And Brian was almost there.

What did he expect to see? Some crazy carnival ride, perhaps? A chimney guarded by a giant mistletoe sprig that would try to eat him alive? Santa's sleigh waiting to take him for a spin?

In the end, it turned out to be a plain wooden door, right smack in the middle of a long terraced building.

Just one of a series of identical entrances, the stone walls black from a century of soot.

"Huh." He looked up and down the facade of the house in front of him. "I'll be damned."

And he reached out to turn the knob.

For some reason, the door to 13 Wellington Road was unlocked, and inside… was just a staircase. Leading ever downwards.

Perhaps the home at this address was a basement one? From here, Brian could barely see six metres down the stairway, so there was no telling how far it went.

"Only one way to find out," he told himself. And set off to discover the truth.

It was a long way down indeed.

Brian quickly lost count of the minutes; it felt like he was descending this staircase for hours—or days—but he knew it couldn't have been quite that long because he had not once needed to stop for a rest.

After all the leg work he had done so far today, he knew his energy would give up very soon.

And yet still he continued going down.

With plenty of time to think about his actions, Brian began to realise just how much he didn't know about what was going on in this town.

I mean, sure, that was what he was trying to discover. But he didn't even know what it was that he didn't know (if that made any sense).

It was always Christmas here, and no one realised the impossibilities of that but Brian. Yet… what did that actually *mean?*

Why had he been led here? What answers could lie at the

bottom of a seemingly endless staircase, and what could he do about them once he learned them?

Everything seemed so suddenly meaningless that Brian began to lose hope. To lose courage. Especially as the night dragged on and on and on, his feet growing heavier as he dragged them down this never-ending staircase.

Just as he wondered if he wouldn't be better served turning around and making the long trek back up, making his way belatedly to Nan and Gramps's house for Christmas Dinner, he found himself at the bottom of the stairs.

The door before him was huge and oaken, looking like one of those dungeon entrances from an old cartoon, or a computer game. A massive iron ring served as a doorknob.

He pulled; the door swung open with a creak.

As it turned out, the room beyond the door was not quite a dungeon. Or, at least, not of the type that Brian might have expected.

No close, cramped, and mouldy walls here. Instead, a massive underground cave had been adapted into a living and working space; machines and furniture shoved into spaces or adapted to fit into certain nooks and crannies along the side walls.

If Brian had to guess, he'd say that the ceiling soared above his head at least a hundred feet—but the light from floor level only reached so high among the jutting rocks up there and it was possible the space reached even further.

No wonder that damn staircase was so long.

Equipment was set up all throughout the haphazard shape of the cavern, doing god only knew what. Huge banks of what looked like computers from the 1960s took up sections of the stone wall, and other more mediaeval contraptions swarmed over others.

Pulleys and wheels and jointed beams of wood were working non-stop, turning and pumping and grinding. The motion was so chaotic that Brian couldn't get a sense of exactly which was doing what and why. Most of the cave floor was empty, but the spaces which were filled were going at it hammer and tongs.

The most unusual aspect to Brian, though, had to be the river.

Sure, caves often had underground rivers flowing through them; the water was likely what formed the caves in the first place. But this one was different.

The fluid rushing through the centre of the stony space was a creamy colour, viscous and hypnotic in its flow. And rather than emerging from some surface inlet, this river was fed from a multitude of tubes.

Yes, myriad wide hoses were suspended from rocky outcroppings, their nozzle-like protuberances spouting the thick liquid to form the fast-flowing river that snaked right down the middle of the space. Each hose was several centimetres in diameter, and though their paths were difficult to trace among the uneven rocks to which they were attached, it appeared to Brian as though the ultimate source of the fluid was the various machine banks along the walls.

At the very end of the river, by one huge flat stone surface, was a turbine—a water wheel. The liquid rushed past the wheel, spinning it faster and faster, though Brian suspected that electricity was not what was being generated here.

There had to be easier ways to power your telly, after all.

And where did all that whiteish liquid go to? It flowed into a crack in the cave wall and out of Brian's sight.

The entire set-up was as bizarre as anything Brian had experienced today. And the day was not yet over.

"Magnificent, isn't it?"

Brian was startled by the sudden voice, coming from over by one particular console bank at a nearby wall. He had not seen the fellow standing there manipulating the levers and dials until his sudden speech drew attention to itself.

For some reason, the man's appearance was a little bit of a letdown. Brian didn't know what he might have expected, but given all the weirdness and the… epic level of this getup in front of him, he supposed he'd rather anticipated a demon—or at least someone disfigured and hiding beneath a mask and cloak.

Very ableist of him, come to think of it. Brian felt a sudden attack of untimely shame.

But no, instead of all of that there was just some chap. Handsome enough, as such things went (as far as Brian could tell, anyway). Dark hair, bit of stubble. Cheeky grin. And dressed in a dull red suit.

The man turned from his work, beaming at Brian, and stuck his hands into his trouser pockets.

"Well," he prompted finally. "What do you think?"

"Er." Brian had no idea what to say, really. "It's… very nice."

The man in red laughed and stepped away from his machine and walked in Brian's direction. "I'll take that at face value, thanks."

He didn't know why he hadn't noticed it before, but this guy had an American accent that seemed out of place in (or even under) such a quaint little British town as… this one.

"What…" Brian cleared his throat, staring at the wonders around him, and then addressed the man in red again. "What is this place?"

Mere feet from Brian now, the other man stopped to spin round, arms held wide in gesture to indicate the vastness of the space they inhabited. "This is Jai-Romaine—or what's left of it. Once the centre of a vast empire, believe it or not. Sad how things turn out, really."

The name meant nothing to Brian, though admittedly his memories were hazy on a lot of things these days.

"And you," he said to the man. "You were what? Its king?"

That elicited an especially wry chuckle from him, though Brian failed to catch the humour in what he had said. "No, no king. Heh. But I do more or less rule over my little household—your town up there." And he pointed to the high, creviced ceiling above them.

Brian looked up at the intricate rock formations, the stalactites with drops of water clinging to their undersides, imagining somehow that he could see his hometown through the metres upon metres of rock.

"Not like a… king." And the man laughed again. "But I like to think of myself as the founder of the place. Head of a family that never stops celebrating the holidays—imagine that! You could say I'm Father Christmas."

The man was no jolly fat man with a beard, but if he indeed had birthed the village shrouded in an eternal

Christmas, then Brian supposed the name more or less fit.

Father Christmas. Bloody hell, this was quite a day.

One thing didn't make sense, though. Actually, a hell of a lot of things, but one that struck Brian in particular at this very moment:

"Why though?"

For a second, Father Christmas seemed thrown for a loop. "Excuse me?"

"All this?" Brian indicated the vast chamber around them. "I mean, what's it all about Alfie?"

"Oh, this old thing?" The man in red waved a hand in self-deprecating dismissal. "Just something I threw together. My little bit to aid the war effort, don't you know."

"War?"

Raising one finger in the air before his face, the other hand shoved deep into his pocket, the man in red seemed to take to the new topic with relish. "Ah, of course: you couldn't possibly know! Thousands of people dying all over the… world. All the time. People you will never meet—*could* never meet. I plan to put all of that to an end."

Brian frowned. "By making it always Christmas?"

Father Christmas grinned even wider. "Genius, ain't it? If I do say so myself." He walked backwards a few steps, gesturing at one of the pipes overhead that carried the pale fluid to the river. "Pure Christmas spirit, Brian old pal. Carried through these tubes, pouring together in this great river. Powering my armies. I've come up with better plans, I admit, but this has gotta be pretty up there."

Not understanding a word of it, Brian frowned. Christmas spirit as a liquid? Powering armies? None of it even *began* to make sense, but it was something else that drew his attention.

"How did you know my name?" He had never introduced himself, yet the man in red had addressed him by name.

"Oh, I know all my children, Brian. What kind of a father would I be if I forgot all of your names?" He walked over to the machine bank with the levers and switches, indicating a row of small security monitors built into the display. "I keep an eye on all of you at all times."

"*All* times?" Brian blushed, thinking about some of the things he got up to at night that he'd rather not be observed doing.

"All times." Father Christmas nodded sagely. "Though a father does know when to give his son a little privacy, don't you worry none."

Somehow that didn't make Brian feel any better.

But none of that was the point, of course. This man here—this self-styled Father Christmas—had enslaved the town above. Made it forever Christmas in some weird plan to support an army that would end a war—presumably by killing the enemy more efficiently.

This had to end. Brian had to put a stop to it. Now!

It was just the two of them here, and he decided to take his chance. Rushing his enemy who had turned his back to look at the monitors on his workstation, Brian suppressed a yell of rage but lifted his fists ready to pummel the fellow in red.

But was stopped by a collection of smaller hands attached to people he had not seen before this moment.

"Oh," the man in red said without turning to look. "You haven't met my minions yet, have you? Say hello, fellows."

All around Brian now was a collection of little men dressed in bright red and green clothes, including floppy knit hats with bells on the end. Underneath those silly head coverings sat ears which ended in points.

They were bloody elves! Santa's elves!

This was getting sillier by the moment.

The looks on the little men's faces, however, were grim and determined. One of them bared gritted teeth as he held Brian back from his assault, revealing that they also ended in little points.

Brian did *not* want those teeth sinking into his flesh. It'd be worse than the sodding candy canes.

"This is crazy!" Brian yelled, straining at his captors' grip in anger. "All of this to win a war? Is it worth it?"

The man in red grew more serious, his eyes almost glowing in fervour as he took a step in Brian's direction. "Not just *win* a war, Brian. *End* a war. All that suffering, all that pain. It could finish, and soon. Isn't that a good thing?"

He seemed sincere, but Brian couldn't go along with his enthusiasm. "You don't get peace through more fighting."

"Peace is exactly what I'm creating, Brian. Peace on Earth, good will towards men. That's what I've created in your town: endless peace. It was my good fortune to find these Lomak generators to turn that good will into something tangible we can use to bring this peace to everyone, everywhere!"

Lomak generators. He seemed to mean the machines creating the liquid that poured into the river beside them.

"Found them?" Brian asked, focusing on odd details as he struggled to find a way out of the grip of the elves that held him captive.

"I'm gonna go with 'found', yeah." Father Christmas smirked, hands back into his pockets now. "Setting them up down here was a real bitch, lemme tell ya. But worth it."

"Nothing could be worth killing over!"

Actually irritated now, the man in red motioned his elves to drag Brian over to the machine back where he stood.

It was a huge console about two metres tall and ten across, the upright portion covered with security monitors and other smaller displays and dials, the desk-like portion that jutted out at waist level covered with faders and switches and levers mostly unlabeled and so complex that Brian had no idea how anyone could make heads or tails of it all.

Father Christmas appeared to however, as he flipped a series of toggles to make the five black-and-white monitors display scenes of people in their homes celebrating Christmas together.

"Look at this, Brian." The man gestured at a scene of an old woman wearing a paper hat pulling a cracker with her grandson, laughing unrestrained as they celebrated the holiday together as a family. "Look at it."

Brian did so, taking it in. All the scenes of Christmas cheer, people enjoying the warmth and good will of the holiday, spending time with friends and family. Loving one another. Having the time of their lives.

"This is what I've done. What you are railing against. Peace, love, understanding. I'm the father of paradise, Brian. What could you find here that you object to?"

He struggled to understand his own argument, but deep inside Brian knew that it was wrong. All of this was wrong.

"You've enslaved them," he said at last, though sounding less sure of himself than before. "Forced them to forget who they are, where they came from. And all to fight your little war."

"Not so little, Brian." The man in red leaned closer and Brian could smell the liquorice-odour of his breath. "Death on a scale you cannot even dream of. Prince Horlat destroys more and more lives every day, and if you think this," he pointed to the monitors, "is enslavement, wait'll you see what *he* does to his captives."

Shaking his head, Brian argued, "A lesser evil is still that. Evil."

Father Christmas sighed, dropping his chin against his chest. "Clearly you're not going to come around to my way of thinking. A pity."

What did that mean? What was he going to do to Brian?

Need to think fast. Find a solution. But what?

What could one man do against all of this? This vastness, this complexity? It was beyond Brian, and he no longer knew why he had ever thought he could do something against it.

But as the elves started to tug him away from Father Christmas, away from the machine that controlled this monstrosity, Brian spotted something.

There was a hole—a gap in the mechanics. Right there amidst the switches. Like a small component had been removed.

And Brian recognised the shape.

Reaching into his coat pocket, he took out the strange

amulet the bearded man on the street had given him. Brian had forgot all about it, but now he saw that its dimensions exactly matched the hole in the console.

Before he could be tugged out of reach, Brian reached forward and placed the amulet in the slot. The man in red saw what was occurring only now at the last moment, and his face transformed into a mask of fury.

Brian only saw out of the corner of his eye, but he could swear that the man's features physically altered, revealing a bestial visage beneath their pleasant covering, but he had no time to contemplate that.

Jutting out from the centre of the amulet was a small protuberance that was now quite obviously a finger-grip, a small lever. And Brian tugged down, felt the switch trip some mechanism inside the unit.

And all hell started to break loose.

As soon as he had pulled on the knob, things began to physically fall apart. Whatever the switch had been designed to do, the apparatus filling this cave did not like it one bit. Hoses which poured fluid into the river sputtered, shook, came free of their restraints.

White liquid began to douse the surroundings, and an ominous creaking sounded from somewhere up above. One of the other console banks sparked, a miniature backfiring noise bursting forth from its inner workings.

And all around the systems of pulleys and fulcrums creaked and groaned, threatening to come to pieces. The giant wheel through which the river ran teetered precariously. One of the computer monitors by Father Christmas's head exploded in a shower of dark glass.

Which is when rocks began falling from overhead.

Brian realised that the entire cave had been part of this complex mechanical system. Tunnels, pipes, and wires became exposed when pieces tore off of the walls—and smoke belched forth from some of the newly-opened fissures.

Rage consuming him, the man in red shook his fists and growled at Brian. "What have you done? You imbecile, what have you done?"

Frightened at the chaos surrounding him, but satisfied with his own actions anyway, Brian turned to the fuming chap in front of him. "Called off Christmas."

The man roared, lunging at Brian, but a chunk of falling rock landed between them causing him to back off before he laid hands on him.

A minor earthquake sent the elves scattering, yelling for their lives. Vanishing into holes Brian couldn't even see. Escaping with their hides intact.

Turning his energy now to the console by his side, the man in red tugged levers, flipped switches, heaved against the dying mechanics.

"Don't quit on me," he commanded the machine. "This isn't over. It can't be over! Christmas must continue."

Brian considered this his best opportunity to make an escape.

As he turned round, however, a pillar of rock with ropes and wooden beams attached to it toppled over and shattered—forming a rubble heap against the door through which Brian had entered the cavern.

His avenue of escape was cut off!

Could he make it out the way the elves had? Frantically, Brian searched for the portals the little men had fled through, but to no avail. He could find no trace of their means of egress.

There had to be another way out. Didn't there?

The cave was so vast, Brian couldn't even see some of the far walls of it. And now with the electric lamps sputtering and failing all around, it became even harder to make anything out in this place.

The wheel at the end of the river finally came loose from its bearings and crashed to the ground, rolling along for several metres before breaking apart and scattering into a million smaller components. A rock fell near Brian's head, and a construction of wood and rope collapsed near his side.

If he didn't do something soon, he was going to die here.

Like Father Christmas over there. The crazed man was still pulling on levers and running his hand along the array of switches and slides on the console. Desperate to salvage his operation, the man paid no attention to the falling debris around him—even when one large rock took out a chunk of the machine right by his left hand.

Brian had to go. But where?

Only one way out that he could see. The white river flowed through a narrow opening in the cave wall—and now that the wheel was out of the way there may be just enough room for him to squeeze through.

Maybe.

And what lay on the other side? For all Brian knew he might find himself in an enclosed space where he would be unable to breathe. Or perhaps end up in a giant vat of liquid with no doorway by which to escape.

But it was his only choice. And so Brian dived into the river.

It smelled of sulphur and—oddly—mint, but he did his best to ignore the odour and swim to safety. A tower of wooden components fell to a crash right beside his position, some of the pieces rolling out to swarm over Brian's head.

He was forced underwater, accidentally gulping down oily-tasting fluid that stung his eyes. As he came back up, something blocked his access to the surface.

Brian panicked, flailing under the milky water, gasping for air and taking in only more of the hazardous fluid.

He couldn't see, couldn't breathe. Up was down and left was right. He had no idea where he was. He seemed to be moving, pushed by the flow of the water, but in which direction?

It didn't take long before he passed out entirely.

⁂

It was six days later, and Brian lay in bed coughing.

Dr Jefferson had given him the OK to come home from hospital two nights ago, but Brian still spent most of the time tucked up in bed. His ordeal had weakened him, and though he was apparently going to be just fine, he sure as hell didn't feel like it.

Whatever that stuff was that he had breathed in, it had done a number on his lungs. No permanent damage, said the doctor, but respiration was going to be difficult for a wee while yet apparently. Brian wished he could just sleep through all of that and wake up when he was done healing.

Sleeping, however, was easier said than done. Not just because of the constant waking up wracked with coughs, but when he *did* manage to drift off, the nightmares took over.

That night, the things he had seen. It all came flooding back, over and over again, when he slept. He had been so sure that he was about to die, with the world collapsing around his ears and white fluid filling his lungs…

Supposedly he'd washed ashore in the stream by the woods, though Brian didn't know how that would be possible. The underground river might have been driven by (broken) machinery, but it couldn't bloody well flow uphill, could it?

How had he made it back to town?

Brian was just starting to reconcile himself to the idea that he would never quite know what had saved his life. In a world filled with talking Christmas cards, biting candy canes, killer trees, underground machines, elf minions, and a guy keeping Christmas alive to further his own war… surviving a possible drowning didn't seem like all that much of a big thing.

Whatever had happened down there in that cavern—and Brian had spoken of it to no one for fear of them supposing him to have brain damage from his experience in the water— it had had the desired effect. From the time Brian had opened his eyes that following day, it was no longer Christmas.

The people of this nameless town were having difficulty coming to grips with all of it, but they more or less carried on with their lives. Looking too closely into the bizarre situation might cause them to learn something frightening, and so it was far easier to just go with the flow and accept the hand they'd been dealt.

What would everyone do now? It was still the holiday season, and not everyone had gone back to work yet. But how would things function once they did? Were any of them even capable of holding down a job? Did they know what that even meant?

They'd soon find out.

"Brian!" It was Nan's voice calling from the other room. She and Gramps had moved in while Brian was recovering, to look after him, and he was grateful for their care and attention. "The bells are going to start soon. You want to come see?"

That's right. It was New Year's Eve. Almost midnight, in fact.

With a groan, Brian got to his feet, grabbing at the crutches propped up against the wall. He still didn't have much strength in his legs, and needed the wooden implements to help him hobble into the living room.

There sat his grandparents next to a little gas heater, glued to the small telly in the corner. A couple of announcers bided their time before the final countdown to the new year, making small talk that they somehow kept from being repetitive for all the hours they'd been on air doing it.

"Oh hello, son," Gramps said as he saw Brian limp into the room. "Didn't know if you was going to miss ringing in the new year wi' us!"

"Never." Brian smiled, and sank into a plush easy chair at the far end of the room. Christmas was over, and wouldn't come again for a whole other year—the way it was supposed to be—but Brian still had his family. Still had his Nan and Gramps to spend the day with, and in that sense he would carry Christmas around with him in his heart.

"Look," Nan said excitedly, "it's starting!"

The last seconds ticked by on the countdown, and then the bells sounded. The two hosts hugged one another professionally, and in the room Brian's grandparents gave each other a happy smooch.

As celebrations sprung up all around the town, party poppers audible from the place next door, Brian had a sudden eerie feeling that caused a shiver to run down his spine.

Why did all of this seem so familiar? These bells, that cheering, these parties?

It was almost like he had done this all before, and not so long ago.

But surely it couldn't be…

FIN

The Yin | *Krystle Kwiatkowski*

Brothers and Sisters,

made of the same blood

forming a bond thicker than water.

However,

not all bonds remain.

Familial and Royal,

ties can be broken by

the use of a lie and sibling betrayal.

A Stone to the Head | *Krystle Kwiatkowski*

The air, freezing to the touch, bites at her pale skin. Snowflakes decorate her raven hair. Her barren feet jam into the snow, which makes them raw and red. She struggles to hold her skirt above the six inches of torture. Her breaths are short and quick as she looks back every few seconds. She doesn't see any animals or people behind.

The young lady stops and stares at the forest around her. There's nothing but pine trees coated in snow; which glistens in the sunlight like it contains little stars. Bumps in the ground are emphasized by the white coat. Her footprints trail in a morphed image of her feet. She tries to orient herself, but it's useless. The trees go on and on making it all appear the same.

A sound, from the left, makes her jump. It sounds like a horse; it's breaths that of one galloping. The young lady snaps her head to look, but there's nothing except … darkness. The shadows made by the sun morph into one. They grow darker and darker 'til it makes the ground pitch black. It covers the trees and, oddly enough, the sky. Nothing pierces through it. What she was once able to see is now hidden. The sound of a horse becomes louder as the darkness grows nearer. Her heart races as she stares at the black mass. It rapidly moves toward her.

The young lady dashes to the right. She manages a few feet before she realizes the darkness is there too. It moves to converge with the other darkness. She tries another direction, but quickly realizes that is unsafe as well. Darkness comes from everywhere; and it's all coming for her. There's nowhere to go. Nowhere to hide.

The sound reaches piercing decibels. She freezes in terror. The young lady pulls the top of her corset away from her body. She thinks maybe if she has a little more room, she'll be able to breathe. Alas, it doesn't work. Darkness is ready to swallow her whole. Panic takes over. She grabs her head and pulls at her hair. Her heart won't slow, she can't stop the darkness. Weight sits on her chest and won't release. In all the madness, the young lady lets out a banshee scream.

***

The young lady opens her eyes. She lays in a bed covered in the finest sheets made by man. Sweat drips down her face. She looks up to the ceiling which tells the story of siblings caught in a fatal feud: Cain & Abel. Right above her is the scene where Cain kills Abel—stone to the head; a personal kill made of envy.

Her arms shake as she props herself up. The young lady takes deep, slow breaths. Her pupils remain dilated. They're stuck on the fireplace at the other end of the room. Flames crackle as they send warmth through the place, though it doesn't reach her. She shivers, still feels the cold from her dream, the air on her skin, the snow underneath her. Everything stays, but she was never there. She was always in her bed under soft blankets—layers of them, in fact.

She stays upright for the rest of the night. As the sun rises, its light pours in. It reveals the seats in the middle of the massive room. Their material looks soft to the touch. You'd melt in them and swiftly fall to sleep if you sat on the cushions. The rug underneath them is green and embroidered with intricate, gold designs. The young lady doesn't admire the sun uncovering it all, though. She remains in a trance. These things are in her eyesight, but she doesn't *see* them. One of her ladies-in-waiting enters the bedroom. She's sad to see the young lady's distress. These nightmares are a nightly occurrence. Have been for months.

The lady-in-waiting approaches the bed. "Princess Anne! You poor girl, you had another nightmare didn't you?"

Anne remains silent. The lady-in-waiting touches her shoulder, which releases Anne from the trance. She turns her head to view the lady. Tears fill her eyes, and they gently fall down her cheek like a caress to comfort her. The lady-in-waiting pulls out a handkerchief from her dress pocket, and wipes off the sweat and tears on Anne's face.

"Come, you must get ready for the ball. You may rest in the carriage since it is a far way to travel."

The lady-in-waiting takes Anne's hand and places her own on Anne's back. She leads her out of the bed. Anne feels weak and fragile; her movements slower than that of the sick elders. Anne removes her nightgown and replaces it with a holiday gown—red velvet with a corset decorated in floral embroidery—gold roses on green stems. They dance around, twisting and turning on themselves. Her hair, once curled, is pinned up high. Anne puts the finest jewels on her hands, ears, and neck.

Anne stares out the giant window as the lady-in-waiting searches through the coat closet. Frost forms around the edges, and snow sits on the outside sill. She watches the carriage, which seems to be holding her father for she can see his silhouette, head out through the castle gates. He's on route to the Christmas Ball, no doubt. A victorious "Yes!" escapes the lady-in-waiting's mouth. She found a grey fur coat, which appears to be very thick and heavy. She carries it as she motions Anne out the door.

Both women make their way down the castle corridor. The lady-in-waiting stays behind Anne, who has perfect posture with her head tilted up and arms at her sides. A young man in riding clothes joins them. His clothes are nicer than that of the stable hands, but not as nice as the royals'. He does, however, share their snobby tone.

He says, "Ready to dance with men who would much rather be in bed with their mistresses?"

"Michael," Anne begins coldly, "how kind of you to visit me on my way out. Tell me, will you be at the ball?"

"I wouldn't miss it for the world," He smirks. "To see everyone glare at my Bastard sister will be quite the Christmas present."

"I am not a Bastard."

Michael chuckles. Anne becomes more rigid in her movements. "As of your Mother's execution, you are," Michael says. "The request was signed by the Pope before her blood even dried."

Anne turns on her heels and glares up at him. She looks deep into his eyes and reaches his soul. Michael doesn't appear fazed. "My blood consists of my mother's, the wife of the King, and my father's, the ruler of England. Yours consists of a chambermaid."

"Yes," Michael begins. He takes pause, "Quite unfortunate *you* and *your* mother's traitorous actions can undo such a royal bloodline."

Michael walks the rest of the corridor, and leaves through the doors on the left. Anne watches as anger builds along with another emotion—pain. The lady-in-waiting helps Anne put on her fur coat. Anne's voice raises and shakes as she speaks.

"My mother and I are innocent. We never betrayed his majesty, the King. We would never do that." The lady-in-waiting rubs Anne's back as they head out the door; held open by a nearby guard, who bows to Anne. Anne removes her gloves and squeezes them—an outlet for her stress.

The carriage ride is quite bumpy. Anne and the lady-in-waiting rock side to side from it. They hear the wheels clink from the pebbles on the ground, and every now and then, a clunk from a dip in the ground. Anne rests her head on the wall as she still squeezes her gloves. She watches the snow on the ground pass through the mini window. The birds fly away when they see the black cart. Everything leaves her, moves far away to escape her. She'd rather be the one escaping—to someplace or someone who would bring her peace. Her mother would do that, but the lies and sins of the court brought her to the hands of an Executioner. A nameless man who, in one swing, chopped her head off in front of a sorrowful crowd, one who believed the Queen betrayed them and their country.

The lady-in-waiting sits across—a good bit away to ensure their legs don't accidently bump each other. Her breaths are deep and uncomfortable. Her hands dance about themselves. She clears her throat and looks over Anne. "Your highness, it may be best to put your gloves on. The winter cold will nip at your fingertips."

Anne doesn't say a word. She remains in her own world—one where the thoughts are dark and lingering, thoughts that clutch her heart and squeezes it with all its might, thoughts that make her want to turn back the clock, thoughts that make her question every fiber of her being.

Her lip quivers. Anne asks, "Have I offended my father? Have I done something to make him believe me guilty of such treasons?"

"Your father loves you," the lady-in-waiting says in a comforting tone.

"Then why doesn't he believe me?" Anne stares down the lady-in-waiting. Her voice rises with the words. A fire ignites, forcing the anger through. "Why does he believe the likes of a crook and a Bastard over me?"

"Petty is not a crook," the lady-in-waiting quickly defends, "he has known the King since their youth and has done many great things for England. As for the Bastard son … you know men, especially *royal* men, are close to their sons whether legitimate or not."

Anne laughs, a little madly. "He was never close to Michael. He always saw him as pushy. Countless times Michael stuck his nose in the King's business, trying to assert a position he never had. Nor does he have the right to have."

She sighs and leans back. The ride gets rockier. The lady-in-waiting places her hand on the seat to keep upright. She clutches her stomach. They enter a road with a field on the left and a forest on the right. Everything is covered in thick snow. It looks heavenly, especially on the green trees.

"My mother did not betray my father, and I certainly did not help her in said betrayals." Anne goes on, eyes glassy. She must release this pain in her chest, reveal the betrayals done unto her. "There were no meetings with the enemy. My mother never plotted against the King or his country. England always came first to her like it does my father.

And I never broke my promise to my betrothed Prince," Anne continues on. "I never laid with another man, or flirted with one even. My reputation is as pure as my heart, which is to say it is innocent."

She waits for the lady-in-waiting to say something. No words spill from her mouth. In fact, she seems to ignore Anne. The Princess returns to the window. Her eyes squint at the sight of a wooden post. Painted on are the words "King's Sorrow."

"Stop the carriage!" Anne shouts. The lady-in-waiting tries to stop her. Anne reaches across and pounds on the wall. "Stop the carriage, at once!"

The horses come to a sudden stop. Anne holds her coat closed as she steps out of the carriage. Her lady-in-waiting grabs her arm to stop her, but her grip is loose. Anne doesn't even notice as she slips out of her grasp.

The driver, an older man with grey hair, meets her. He bows to her as the lady-in-waiting joins them. Like her, he seems confused by Anne's request.

"Is there a problem, your highness?"

"You are going the wrong way."

"Excuse me?"

"I may not know my way around these parts very well, but I do know that this is not the way to Thurlow Castle. Thurlow Castle is to the right of this land, and as I can tell by the post we have gone left. We must turn around."

"With all due respect, your highness," the driver starts, "I am going where the King has instructed me to."

"I'm confused," Anne thinks aloud. "Why would his majesty tell you to go there. There's nothing there but the jails and scaffold used for executions."

Anne reads everyone's face. The driver and lady-in-waiting both look sad as if they're hiding a truth that now dawns on Anne. She can no longer hide the tears. They begin to fall slowly, which makes her eyes red.

"No," She gasps at her lady-in-waiting. "No, no, no, no!"

The lady-in-waiting grabs hold of her arm … tighter this time. The guards, who were following behind in another carriage, step out due to the commotion. Anne frantically looks around. Her only place to run is the forest. Maybe she can lose them. Maybe they'll be close behind. Who knows? She knew she'd have to ditch the heavy coat, though. Her heels will surely hinder her efforts, too.

She drops her gloves and yanks her arm away from her lady-in-waiting. Anne begins her run, tosses her shoes away and rips off the fur coat in the process. She hikes up her skirt as she goes deep into the forest. Her feet take her between the trees. The unusual pattern will confuse the guards.

The guards are heard close behind. They call out, "Anne! Get back here!" Their voices strike fear into Anne. They're gonna be the death of her. If they find her, they're going to take her to her grave. She looks back, obsessively. They can't find her. They can't!

The soles of her feet become sore. They're red from the cold and rough ground. The voices become quieter and quieter—silence. She can only hear the sound of her quick breaths. Anne stops for a moment to try to figure out her location. She's lost … just like in her dream.

Panic sets in. Anne pulls the top of her corset away from her body. More room, easier breathing, right?

Anne brushes some of her fallen hair out of her face. She must decide which way to run. Forward like she has? Should she throw them off and go right? Or is left the safe way?

Suddenly, a horse is heard from the left. It's galloping. Anne turns and finds Michael, who approaches her at high speeds. He makes her decision for her: right it is. Anne lifts her skirt back up and runs. Unfortunately, Michael is faster. When his horse is close enough, he hops off and continues on foot. In what seems like seconds, Michaels grabs hold of Anne. He drags her back to the horse. She wails as she pulls her entire body away from him. He's much too strong for her.

Anne pleas, "Let me go! Let me go!" Tears spill from her eyes. Michael doesn't seem to care. It's as if he enjoys the pain she's experiencing. The hurt. The betrayal. Everything. "I'm innocent, I beg of you!"

She pulls with all her might. Michael yanks her toward him and holds both of her wrists together. He smiles a wicked smile. "I know."

Anne's eyes go wide. A gasp escapes her throat as he throws her onto the horse. Her stomach lays across the saddle, her legs free to kick, which they do. Her cries become more intense, though she knows there's no use. Michael hops onto the horse and runs off into the direction of King's Sorrow.

When they get there, Anne has since composed herself. As guards escort her to the scaffold, her face remains stone. Her eyes focus on the place she is to stand—in front of everyone with red eyes and pained feet. She is to forgive the Executioner for what he is to do to her. Anne will kneel and lay her head down—bowing down to the King, his majesty, one final time as she leaves the world by the edge of a sharp sword.

Empty | *Sam Baker*

You asked me to explain empty.
Maybe I'm wrong, but empty doesn't feel
like anything worth explaining;

it's just empty—broken,
unable to feel whole again,
wishing there was an end to this pit I fell in.

Empty is me—washed out, scared,
pinned down by the weight of nothingness
because I know what used to be there.

Empty is the hollow core of a body
begging to be filled with love, purpose,
anger, anything, but the only thing is empty.

My heart is a rock falling through the cavern
of my chest with nothing to keep it there,
tell me it's mine, make me feel alive. Empty.

You asked me to explain empty, but I can't.

How do you explain a hole that can never be filled?

Honest Christmas | Sam Baker

On the first day of Christmas, my true love gave to me cold sores and crippling depression. Two for the price of one is a good deal I'd say. One day, I was inhaling the fumes from the tea which hovered under my nose. It was a dangerous scent that reminded me of something old, but the hint of fresh honey made it feel new. It's amazing how many new things we can ruin.

I held the mug between my hands, brushing my thumb along the chipped edge, not sipping because I hated the taste of tea but liked the thought of pretending to drink tea. It was a ritual—like lighting a cigarette but not actually smoking. I did it for the motion, the warmth, to give myself something familiar and concrete in a world full of the constantly changing.

Hammer was the reason I held the tea. He was my familiar thing. He was the compass in my life which felt like a really long episode of *Lost*. I was twenty when he died, and he was twenty two. Most people don't believe me when I tell them that. Dogs aren't supposed to live past their teens, but Hammer did. I had a cousin who got sick right after she graduated high school. She was going to attend college in Finland when she got better. She was going to waste her life away in med school to be a doctor who looks at feet all day, but she never got better, and even Hammer outlived her.

I can still hear the conversation in my head right now. My mom was chasing me down the hall to the garage, the slap of her sneakers on the hardwood made it feel like someone was pounding on the door, trying to break down the shell of silence I had created. Dad tip-toed down the hall behind her as if he didn't want to be involved in the conversation but just wanted to watch.

Mom didn't hold her hands on her hips when she was mad like some moms do. She'd scrunch the sides of her dress in her fists like a ball. She always wore a dress. Sometimes I thought of those scrunched up wads of floral fabric inside her fists as eggs, and I'd sit and wait for them to crack as she squeezed tighter and tighter. But something else was breaking that day as I took Hammer into the garage and gave him a bowl of water. Mom's words were breaking the peace I tried to find within the small space between the washing machine and the wall of my dad's racing bikes.

"He's so old. How are you going to bring him here and expect him to survive?" she began.

Her voice climbed to a higher pitch when she talked, but she never got louder. She always started the conversation off as loud as she would ever get. She was like a tea kettle that was ready the moment it touched the stove. But I couldn't quiet her by turning off the heat. There was no way to quiet her at all. She was a self-soothing kettle, and I just had to wait for her to go silent on her own.

"I'm not paying his bills. I'm not gonna buy him food. You'll have to get a job to take care of him," she continued as she realized I wasn't going to respond.

"I know Mom," I said as I rolled my eyes.

"You should have just left him there. Looks like he only has a few hours," she said as she looked at the drooling, overweight, blind dog with a scowl.

That's the thing about my mom. She always had to scowl when she was judging someone. It made for an awful poker face. But I knew she was judging Hammer because he didn't matter to her. But more so, she probably loathed him because he mattered more to me than she did. And she just couldn't stand anyone loving an old, nearly dead dog more than her.

"And look, he's already making a mess," she said as she yanked on the drool covered rug he was standing on.

He rolled on the ground in a dramatic way as she tugged the floor out from beneath him. And he just sort of lay there like a beached whale, an overturned turtle, anything but a dog. And he huffed like his life was hard, which it was because he was eighteen then and still trying to buy more time. His warm, quick, and slobbery breath left a puddle on the ground beside him where he sprawled out and simply existed within the garage of mine.

"It's fine," I said to Hammer as I watched my mom attempt to shake his drool off the rug and then angrily toss it into the broken laundry basket.

"And I sure as hell am not digging a hole in my new garden to put this thing in the ground when it dies," she said in one last defiant threat, knocking her head back as if she expected me to be afraid.

But I was as scared as a lion might be about a wasp that stung its side. I was annoyed, but I could never truly be afraid of a small and buzzing thing like that. She was so insignificant in my worries that I didn't even think twice about letting Hammer chew on one of her favorite towels after she left. I looked at Dad for a response as she pushed past him in the doorway. He just shrugged and moved on. That man shrugged through his whole life.

Don't be upset that I put Hammer in the garage. I slept there too, so he wasn't alone. I lived in the garage, walled in by the washing machine and laundry baskets. I had been living there so long that my mom turned my room in the house into an art gallery, a place for her beloved oil paintings of horses; the ones she felt were more expressive than me.

That night, I hefted Hammer onto the mattress with me, his body like a cannon ball leaving a dent beneath his weight. And I don't know if he could really hear me, but I hummed Christmas songs to him under my breath as I laid Mom's towel beneath the stream of drool that seeped out of his jowls like a broken sprinkler. We shared a blanket too, his warmth making my face red beneath the cool air in the poorly insulated garage. And he was such a large dog that I almost imagined this is what it might be like to sleep with a man beside me in bed, to reach over and feel the realness of someone else's body. Hammer was my first true love, but not the one who gave me cold sores.

That night when I closed my eyes, I could hear my parents talking to each other in hushed voices. They were yanking clothes out of the dryer on the other side of the garage. Mom's stockings were tangled around a pair of Dad's pant legs. I could hear her picking the knots apart with her fingers, and the drip of the leaky washing machine made harmony with this noise.

"She needs to take that thing back," mom said as the sounds of clothes tumbling into a basket drowned out her voice.

Dad didn't say anything, but I guessed that he just shrugged as they left the room and closed the door quietly behind them as if they were suddenly worried they'd wake me. I laughed to myself as I thought of my mom's words. I couldn't take Hammer back to the shelter even if I wanted to.

I saw him there earlier that day in a slump in the corner of his cell. I call them cells because that's exactly what they looked like. It was a concrete room with bars on the front, no sort of blanket to keep him warm, and no other dogs to keep him company. And I knew for no other reason than the fact that I overheard the volunteers chatting, that Hammer was about to die.

He wasn't going to die because his body was giving out on him, because he had cancer or a disease of any sort. He was going to die because he was old, and they decided his time was up. I didn't like the fact that someone other than fate could decide that Hammer was done living. They really gave me no choice.

I would have gone through all the paperwork and paid the adoption fee of forty-two dollars for the elderly residents, but there wasn't time. I was sixteen, and I read on a form in the front office that no one under eighteen could adopt an animal on their own. I would have to convince my parents to sign the papers and take him home, and I knew that wasn't going to happen. So I took him.

I just opened the cage when the volunteers were in the other room, and I ran. He ran too although I'm not sure he could actually see where we were going. But I could see, and that was all that mattered. We were going home. I didn't know anything about him other than the fact that his name was Hammer and he was eighteen.

I was just a kid then, so I didn't know, but I thought that stealing a dog from a shelter was something I could go to jail for. So Hammer, the runaway death row inmate, became mine, and I dressed him as a fat, round candy cane for Christmas.

On the first day of Christmas … well you know … the cold sores … and later depression. We'll start with the cold sores first. It's always good to start with your small problems first. Because if you try to fix the big things, they turn into little things, and all those little things will fall into a big mess on your lap, and you'll have no idea how to put it all back together.

The cold sores were annoying blemishes that stuck to my skin like a birth mark or mole. And like a mole, I felt like they would never go away. I'm not going to tell you I was attractive then. Of course I could tell you that and you wouldn't know if I'm lying or not. But this is Honest Christmas. So honestly, I was a train wreck, and the cold sores were the cherry on top of the disaster sundae that was my face. I should have given my true love glasses for Christmas so that he wouldn't have gotten close enough to give me cold sores.

How exactly do you get a cold sore? Well when a mommy and daddy love each other very much … no not that one. When two people put their lips together in what's called a kiss, (sometimes tongues too, but that's not vital to the equation), and when one of those people have the red, annoying splotch of irritated skin which can usually be found in the corner of their mouth, then they give it to the other person. It's a love gift, something a lot more manageable than a baby, but still just as annoying.

So there I was, looking down at my tea, wondering if it would taste better with something more bitter inside it, and my true love swooped in with a mouth full of cold sores and kissed me. I knew what was going to happen from the beginning, and I accepted it. It was a small causality of love, one of the bearable kinds anyway.

My true love had a name, but I didn't like to think of him that way anymore. But once he didn't have a name. Once he was just a man. That's right … a man. This is no teenage, high school sweetheart, marry me and grow old together love story. He was a man who carried no importance to me other than the fact that his dog liked my dog. That's sort of how all the things in my life worked out, by coincidence. I don't know about God, or fate, or some higher power toying with my life as if it was a game. But if there really was someone molding my life like a sculptor, I was a big mistake which they tried to pass off as intentional so they wouldn't have to feel bad about themself.

But this man who was dragged by his brown pit bull across the dusty field of the old dog park, the man who was bending over, catching his breath as he tried to calm the excited beast within his grasp, he looked at me like he didn't mind looking at me. And I didn't mind looking at him, even with the cold sores. Most of the time it's as simple as that. There aren't any sparks other than a few in your gut that could also have just been dinner from earlier that night. It was the firework equivalent of a sparkler stick. And for the most part, there's never a good way to explain why you like looking at this person so much. It's just one of those biological things that most of us try to avoid thinking about because it's too complicated to understand.

Some people will try to say that looks aren't important, but they're wrong. Whether or not your true love is 'gorgeous' doesn't matter. They just have to be your kind of 'gorgeous'. He was my kind of gorgeous, and I only hoped I was his. The bulk of a relationship is based on hope; hope they don't hate my voice, hope they like this song, hope they don't leave me after meeting my parents, hope they don't leave me at all, hope they don't hate the holidays, hope they don't mind cold sores.

It was November one year, before the cold sores and the first day of Christmas. It was right after Thanksgiving in that awkward between-the-holidays time when things don't feel 'normal' but still haven't picked up that warm holiday spirit again. That's the last 'hope' moment I can remember. We were with each other for a few months or years at this point; I'm not sure because it all seemed like one long week. We were picking out a Christmas tree.

His parents were supposed to join us, but they couldn't make the drive because of the snow. And I was secretly happy about this. I even had to hide my smile behind the puffy scarf that smelled like the apple cider I spilled on it earlier that day.

He hadn't met my parents and never would. It seemed only right that I stay in the dark about his as well. I didn't want any sort of reminders about what he would look like when he grew older. Age was a forbidden subject when we were together. I honestly didn't know how old he was, but he looked young like me, so I didn't care about not knowing.

It's not that we specifically made a rule for not talking about our age and getting older, watching as our bodies turn on us with each crease and grey hair, getting one more day closer to shopping for coffins for each other; It just wasn't something we did.

I don't think much about death for a reason, a reason that seems obsolete now. But when I have considered it, I decided that I don't want to be buried in a cemetery or put in an urn on someone's mantle. I want to be buried in some stranger's backyard, so when their dog digs a hole to hide his bone, he'll find a pile of even more bones as if he struck gold. I would do it for Hammer, but he's dead. I do think that would make someone's day to play fetch with their dog and realize that they're holding a human femur. It might be terrifying at first, but it would be a great story to tell at parties.

The Christmas trees we were looking at that day were kind of like bones. He said it had to be the perfect one, but I knew there weren't many good choices in this batch of miniature trees that stood in rows in the supermarket parking lot, sitting in a pile of their own needles as if the cold made their skin fall off. I felt like the cold was going to make my skin fall off too.

I feel like I learned the most about him then as I watched him watch the trees. He was careful as he looked at each one. I studied with him as if I knew what to look at, but I was clueless as I curled my toes inward to keep them warm. It was as if we were picking out a new car, or ordering a grill online. It had to be the right one, had to fit all of our needs for the best price. And we were not going to settle for anything less than a good deal.

It was because he was so adamant about choosing the right tree, that I noticed when his eyes wavered. And like a dog, heeding to the signal of its master, I looked too. There are so many things that could have happened which would draw his attention away from the important task of choosing a dead plant to stick in our house. But this one was something that made my chest feel like it was full of cold water, so full that I couldn't breathe.

There was a woman standing there in front of us. And to me, it didn't look like she was standing, but floating. I'm sure that's what my true love thought too. Her feet were no doubt planted onto the ground among the piles of pine needles, but the flow of her long grey cardigan and the toss of her wavy hair made her seem like someone who wasn't meant to stand on the ground.

She reminded me of the Ghost of Christmas Past. The glow that surrounded her skin was angelic, heavenly, and I couldn't help but wonder if she was there to show me all the things I tried to forget from long ago. But I knew that she wasn't there for me.

I couldn't even see her face, but my true love's eyes were locked on her like he hadn't seen a creature so rare. And I felt small in comparison although the woman was at least a few inches shorter than me. But the way he looked at her gave me a new sense of doubt, one that dug a hollow trench in my conscious in a place that was once filled with trust. He looked at her like he didn't mind looking at her. He looked at her as if he knew she wouldn't mind growing old with him. This is the last 'hope' moment I remember. *I hope he doesn't forget me.*

We weren't always a couple who tried desperately to hold onto those small bits of hope. There was happiness in there somewhere. We found it again for a short while as we brought the wilting tree into our apartment (the best kind of deal we could find in town), and decorated it with paper dolls and strings of red streamers. And I even found myself laughing as I reached to tie the bow on top of the tree and True Love danced his fingers across my exposed belly where I was the most ticklish.

We were surrounded by happiness everywhere in our home. As long as we didn't step out of that door, it would stay that way. True Love's dog, Stan, played along with the Christmas game as we dressed him in the holiday sweater with snowmen and candy canes embroidered into the sides. And that dog who once wouldn't let me touch him, panted in excitement as I scratched underneath his belly.

He wasn't Hammer. No dog would ever be like Hammer. But Stan was still a good dog who deserved love. So Stan, True Love, and I curled in a big lump on the couch that night and watched *A Christmas Carol* on VHS tape. And we were happy like that, to pretend that this moment was the only one that mattered, that this place with just us and our dog, surrounded in each other's warmth like I once was with Hammer, was the place we were meant to stay forever. It was a good dream, but all good dreams come to an end. The end of mine started with that phone call.

I jumped at the sound of my cell ringing from across the room. It sat on the kitchen counter, vibrating against a bottle of Sparkling Cider so it made a clinking noise with each buzz. I paused the movie as I pried myself out of the couch, not wanting to miss anything even though I'd seen it nearly thirty times before. And I answered the phone with a quick breath as I noticed who was calling. The number was my parents' house phone. I usually would have let it go to voicemail, but I was feeling happy that night, happier than I had been in a while.

"Teri?" my dad said on the other line.

Sometimes it was like he didn't know who he was calling. I hated when he asked like that, as if he was the one answering. His voice sounded dull like always. And I was sure his words were going to be slow, as if he had just woken up from a nap. That's how he always sounded, as if he wasn't sure where he was going with the sentence yet, so he gave himself time to catch up.

"Yeah?" I asked as I tapped my fingernails on the empty glass bottle in front of me.

As I waited for my dad to respond, I wondered how hard I would have to squeeze the bottle for it to break. I even wrapped my hand around the neck of the bottle to test it, but I let go when my knuckles turned white because I didn't want to clean up the mess if it were to shatter. I had to resort to letting my mind flow like this when I talked to my dad. I needed something to fill the void between the words so I wouldn't go insane within the silence.

"Something happened," he explained.

Something … not nothing … but something. My dad was a clever guy, trying to disguise bad new as something simple. But I knew that he was lying to himself, trying to lie to me with that fake sense of calmness that he tried to pass off as genuine. But to me, he just sounded like a scared little kid, afraid to tell his mom he fucked up.

"What is it?" I finally asked as I realized he wasn't going to keep talking.

I was used to waiting like that because Mom always had something to add onto her sentences. It was always one run-on after another after another, and I couldn't tell if we were still talking about the same thing or had started something else entirely. I wasn't used to talking to my dad as much. I guess he didn't know when to keep talking, so I led him. It almost felt as if after all these years, I, the daughter, was teaching him the art of conversation.

"Mom was in an accident. She was hit by a truck. She didn't make it," he finally blurted out so suddenly as if he were afraid of the words.

I could hear his sobs flow after, but they were so quiet that they could have just been shrugs. I liked to think that he was just shrugging because I had never heard Dad cry like that before. It was so ghostly the way it seeped out of his chest, crawling through the speaker into my ear. I almost wanted to drop the phone then for fear of a haunted mind. But with the direness of what he just said, the unfamiliarity of his words, the way they sounded like another language as I thought about them again, I knew I had to stay there.

"She's dead," he said as if he had to explain the meaning behind his words to me.

But his words didn't paint the right picture because Mom didn't just drive. She held one hand on the wheel and one foot pressed firmly on the pedal as she painted her makeup onto her face in the mirror. She used to always say *that mirror* was the best one for putting on mascara. So she'd hold her mouth wide open as she brushed her lashes with the black gunk, flipping her gaze back and forth from the mirror to the road, swearing to herself that she was a safe driver to make herself feel better for indulging in the vanity of putting her appearance before the basic rules of driving.

And I could have imagined that she wasn't just in an accident but a wreck, one that left her neck and spine all crumpled. And I knew that it was probably more than a truck—a semi, going downhill with nothing to stop it but my mom's powder blue Prius. I let out a jagged breath, wondering if Mom's last one sounded the same.

"You home?" I asked.

I wasn't sure if he was at the hospital or not.

"I'm home," he paused, and I could have guessed it was because he was busy shrugging. "Listen, the funeral is on Saturday at two … at the old church … see you there," he said in slow whisper as if he was falling asleep.

"Okay," I said.

I pulled my thumb to the 'end call' button, but my dad beat me to it, and the screen of my phone flashed red as the call details appeared in front of my face. In one minute and thirty two seconds, I learned all I needed to know about my mom. She was dead … that was who she was now.

I jotted down the date and time for the funeral on a sticky note like just another routine thing that I stuck to the fridge next to the grocery list. And I etched the letters carefully as I pulled the address of my old church out of the recesses of my mind. I told myself I would go, that if I wrote it down, I would go, but as I walked away from the fridge and back toward the living room, I honestly knew that I wouldn't. Why I wouldn't go, that truth was too hard to uncover that night.

"Who was that?" my true love asked as I fell back into the couch and hit play on the remote.

"My dad," I said casually as I shoved a handful of salty popcorn into my mouth, feeling the kernels crunch between my molars, lodging themselves into my gums.

"About that … sorry my parents couldn't make it today. But I've been thinking it'd be good for you to meet them. And I really think it's time for me to meet yours," he said as he reached his arm around my shoulders, something he had never done before.

"That's not going to happen," I said as I shook my head.

But at the time, I felt so emptied of emotion that I didn't know how to properly show my distress.

"I know you don't want me to meet them. But I think it's been long enough. And once we get it over with, we won't have to do it again for a long time," he encouraged me as he squeezed my arm with the haze of whiskey still fresh on his face.

"My mom just died, so it's not going to happen," I said as I pulled his arm off my shoulder and sat forward on the couch.

I felt like a dry faucet. I should have been full of something, anything that would have made this situation unbearable, but I just … wasn't. His eyes grew wide, that sort of wide look that makes you want to stab out your own eyes with needles so you don't have to see it haunting you again. I shivered as I turned my face away.

"I'm sorry," he began as he sat up and ran his hand on my back. "Are you okay?" he added as he tried to catch my gaze with his.

"I'm fine," I said as I turned the T.V. off and stretched up from the couch.

The rest of the night was quiet. No matter where I went, what I did, he was lingering behind me, watching me as if he was ready to pick me up if I were to fall apart. But I wasn't breaking, or cracking, or even wearing under the pressure of this heavy news. The only cry that left my body that night was when I stubbed my toe on the edge of the dresser in the bedroom.

"I don't get it," he said as he tossed his wet hair with a towel while he stood in the bedroom doorway.

"What?" I asked as I kept my eyes on the book that I was reading while I sat in bed.

"Your mom just died. Aren't you sad?" he asked as he tossed the towel into the hamper just like my mom used to.

I knew he tried to seem curious, but his voice sounded pained. I shrugged but didn't speak because I didn't know how to feel yet. I didn't want my voice, which had betrayed me before, to decide that now. So I bit my tongue and waited until he crawled into bed. And as I sat my book down and turned the light off, I could feel the coolness blanket my body. This was the first night I wasn't warm with True Love beside me, and it made me miss Hammer even more.

The days after were bleak. They weren't painful, or filled with pity and hatred, they were just days that felt heavy with something that I couldn't quite explain—it was in my body, heavy like sand filling up my legs, so heavy that sometimes I couldn't walk. And the nights that followed were empty … empty and cold.

The week following up to my mom's funeral felt like one long day. And I lived that day sleeplessly, hoping for it to be over soon. At the end of that day, when my dad would be following my mom's coffin down the road in his old pickup truck, I sat at my kitchen bar and stared at the refrigerator. There was a note on the fridge door, the one that carried the address of the last place my mom would be before she was put in the ground.

I tiptoed to the door of the fridge and read the note again, trying to feel the weight of the letters hit my chest the right way. But like last time, it was just a note that disappeared among the wall of reminders to pick up apples and dish soap.

True Love waited for me at the door, but I just shrugged when he asked me if I was ready to go. I knew then why Dad shrugged all the time. It was easier than saying something I'd regret. It was easier than walking out that door and following the address on that sticky note. I guess I didn't know True Love as well as I thought. He left without me. And I stood in the middle of the room, staring at the door while he went to meet my mom for the first time.

I got lost within a dream that I wasn't sure was just a dream. I saw True Love standing there in front of my dad. His hair was combed back like it was when he just left. And he stood there, hesitantly stepping forward as if he didn't know where to begin. 'Hello … I'm your daughter's … whatever. She couldn't come, but I'm here. I know you don't know me, but I want to know you. I'm sorry I didn't get to know her too," he'd say as he nodded over to my mom.

He would have cared about things like that. He would have wanted to make my dad happy even if I couldn't. And I wasn't sure if anything could make my dad happy at that point, but I liked to think that my true love would try. I smiled and wanted to cry at the same time as I thought about his bravery, stepping out into the cold world, walking up into a funeral for a woman he didn't know, expecting somehow to fit within the crowd. Or maybe he didn't expect to fit in. Maybe he knew that people would judge him as a stranger.

My mom wasn't nice to me, but she was nice to other people. And those other people were only nice to a select group of people just like her. They had their clique, their crowd. They had their family that wasn't family. And within that family was the bitterest, most toxic people I have ever met.

I couldn't imagine True Love standing by Sarah who went to the salon each week for touchups so no one would know she's just an old hag, clutching onto her youth by the dollars in her purse. Or maybe he'd be by Hailey who always used a napkin to open doors, (even the ones in her house), so she wouldn't catch the monster germs from the other women's monster children.

Or maybe he'd sit in the pew next to Stacy and her five young boys, the calmest and most careful children I've ever met. Sarah always talks about how Stacy's husband is rough with the kids and that's why they don't talk much. But I know it's just because Stacy is a mom who likes quiet. Her kids know that when mom is happy, their whole world is much better.

But Stacy let's Sarah spread the rumors because she doesn't care about Sarah or any of the other women there. She just cares about my mom. In fact, she might have wondered why she even came to the mess of a funeral anyway. She wouldn't even want to go up to the casket for fear that she might see more of my mom than she wanted.

But truthfully none of those tacky bitches really mattered. That's what Mom would have said. The only thing that matters is that Mom's hair is done up well and her makeup on right how she likes it. Dad would have made sure they got that right. Because my mom was the only bitch who mattered that day, and she wasn't going to let any of the others outshine her. Maybe it's best I didn't go. I might have run the risk of throwing her off her throne.

I imagined True Love sitting there, but I couldn't understand what would have been going through his mind then. What could you be thinking then when you hear strangers talk about another stranger and you're supposed to pretend to be sad? Maybe he actually was sad. I don't know. There were a lot of things I realized I didn't know about him then.

But maybe he was just thinking about nothing. They say opposites attract. My mind is always busy, winding through different thoughts, scenarios, images, and trying to figure out which I should spend the most time thinking on. Maybe he just sat there without thinking about anything. Maybe he felt just as empty as I was. Maybe he went to the funeral to get full. It's like he was waiting in line at a buffet with an empty plate in his hands. He was empty, hungry, and ready to address his basic human needs. Was grief a need?

It was late when he got back, but I didn't realize how much time had passed because I was standing in the same spot, staring at the door, begging myself to move. But I was just the shell of a person who once knew what it meant to have purpose. All of that had washed away now. I was a vacant body, waiting for someone to come and move me; place me in a spot I belonged, among important things that would give my life some sort of meaning.

He was quiet as he walked in. He took off his scarf and hung it on the back of the chair, throwing his snow covered jacket over it. I became his shadow as he walked through the house and took off his outfit bit by bit—shoes by the fireplace to keep warm, socks over the hamper to dry, shirt and pants back in the closet because he didn't wear them for that long.

And like a routine, he got into his sweats, I pulled the baggy hoodie over my head, and we found ourselves in bed, curled together like one body so we could share the warmth. Our bed felt like home again, and even though this night was the worst night to be happy, I found myself smiling as I felt his chest rise and fall against my back.

One thing I wish my true love gave me was more hope. But he gave me depression, which preys on wild hopeful thoughts. He gave me a gift I couldn't return, one I felt like I was stuck with forever. It wasn't like that at first. At first I thought there would be a light at the end of the tunnel or some bull shit like that. It always sounds like bull shit, but it's worth believing because what else are you going to do? You aren't going to try to criticize the thing that's giving you hope. So sure it's a light that I was waiting for, some sort of sign that things were going to be alright, that I wasn't going to be stuck much longer, that I was going to survive.

But the light didn't just appear one day. I had to work for it. I thought I would find that hope eventually if I kept going. But one day I realized that I was lost in the dark. And I ran out of hope of finding hope. I realized then that everything I had done to try and get better, all the times I kept searching for that light was useless because it just made me even more lost. My attempts became failures. I became pointless. Life sucks and then you die. That's depression. And it hit me like a semi-truck going downhill with nothing to stop it but me.

All of that started on Christmas Day, a week after the funeral, when my true love bent over my cup of tea and gave me cold sores. I wasn't even expecting it. It was the mistletoe that I remember seeing first. I thought of how cheesy it was that he was kissing me under the mistletoe, but now I wish I would have stayed there longer. But the fire was getting too warm on my face, so I turned away from the hearth and toward the room.

A pile of his bags met me there in the hallway, and I squinted at them as if they were in a different language, like if I looked at them long enough, I could crack the code. But there was no cracking this code. There was just confusion, just anger, just a silent but helpless plea as I watched him try to grab the handles of each bag.

"What's this?" I asked as I casually tried to block the hall.

I say casual, but inside I was frantically running around, trying to remember if there was something I did wrong, something I should be sorry for. But he just pulled his bags onto his arm and shook his head like he didn't know how to begin the words, the ones he didn't want to say.

"Why didn't you go?" he asked.

I stepped back in shock. I knew he was talking about her funeral. I didn't need to ask for him to explain, but I wanted to so I could stall for just a little longer. The question he was asking wasn't something I was ready to answer. I didn't know if I would ever be.

"That's why I'm doing this Teri," he began as if he realized I wasn't going to answer. "I need some time away. I need to see my parents, to remember what's important. I need *you* to remember what's important," he said as he looked at me desperately and gathered Stan's leash in his free hand.

I should have said his name then. I should have shown him that I wasn't afraid to love him. I should have told him the truth about how I felt. He looked scared, like he didn't know if I had anything left to give him. And the way he swayed back and forth in the hall, looking for a path around me, it made me feel like he was a prisoner that I didn't want to imprison. I didn't understand how my indifference could affect someone like this. I didn't know what to say, but I knew I had to say *something*.

"I don't know," I finally said.

I lied because it was better than thinking about why I didn't want to be there to see my mom again. I could understand if I really tried. But I didn't want to. I didn't want to understand death, a thing that I intentionally treated as an unwelcome guest. I didn't want to think about being there, staring down at my mom's pale and powdered face. I lied because I didn't want to imagine looking into her casket and seeing myself there looking back. But most of all, I lied because I didn't want him to know that I … just … didn't … care. Honesty was worse than letting him go.

He gathered his dog and his bags in one big heap surrounding his body. And he nodded as he pushed past me in the hall as if he knew what I was doing. I was telling him that my pride was more important. It was like he knew I would try to forget his name, try to forget the way he made me feel, try and try to get rid of his cold sores. But the fact that he walked out that door so quickly made it harder to watch him go. And I just watched …

When I heard the door shut, that bolt click, I felt full again. I wasn't empty anymore. I was full of tears that I didn't know I had. I was full of grief that I didn't recognize. I was full of hate for the parting. But it was my true love that made me cry, not the void my mom left. That's why he walked out the door because I couldn't care about her.

What did he see at that funeral? Did he know the truth that I wouldn't tell him? Did he know that I didn't care? Could he see it on her face, how much I didn't love her?

It was True Love leaving me then that reminded me life wasn't fair. He left me alone on Christmas Day, a day that I loved for no other reason than the fact that I loved it, just like I loved him. And now it had turned sour. And as I looked at those boxes sitting by the fireplace, the ones that I left for him to open, I couldn't help but think that they belonged in the trash. This was the day I tried to forget his name. I scratched it off each box and wrote 'TRASH' over it instead. Those boxes that sat there by the fireplace carelessly wrapped in brown paper bags, topped with a homemade bow, they remained unopened, their owner having abandoned them. It was the first time I felt like I could empathize with a box because I felt abandoned too.

I usually went out to walk in the snow and build miniature snowmen each Christmas Day, but I was in no condition to leave the house then. This year, I would break tradition. The cats and mice wouldn't get their snowmen this year because I was too broken to think about childish things like that. I had despair to think about, or rather ignore.

So I just lay on the couch, becoming a part of the cushions as my body sunk deeper and deeper into it as the hours passed. I let *A Christmas Carol* play on repeat, and it helped to drown out my thoughts, the ones that were so loud they were giving me a headache. I went back and forth from thinking that True Love was like Scrooge; to thinking that I was more like the grumpy old man who could be blamed for all the things that went wrong on Christmas.

That's the frustrating thing about how it all happened. It wasn't just his fault. I couldn't blame it all on him. I couldn't just throw it into 'not my fault' valley and forget all about it as if it was just an unfortunate thing this cruel world gave birth to. Because True Love and I gave birth to this mess on our own. We were the parents of this betrayal, this loneliness. We were the founders of this feeling of sorrow that I now suffered. I wondered if he suffered too.

The days after my true love left felt like a game. I was counting, counting all the reasons he left, all the reasons I was glad he was gone. And it was a game because I knew it wasn't true. But I had to convince myself it was, so I could forget that it was my fault I was alone. So instead of finishing my pile of client work for the holiday, I made a list.

On the second day of Christmas my true love gave to me a reason to hate myself. I felt fine when he was here. But once he left, I roamed through the empty house, with no paw prints following behind me. And I actually started to miss Stan. I missed him almost as much as I missed True Love. And I knew they would both still be there if I had just been honest.

On the third day of Christmas, my true love gave to me a sink full of dishes. They weren't his dishes, but mine. True Love was always the one to wash the dishes. He said it was his form of therapy. So I eagerly handed him my dish each night so he could scrub away his grief. But the sink was full now with a stack so tall that one more spoon might knock it over.

On the fourth day of Christmas, my true love gave me an empty stomach. I couldn't add one more dish onto that mountain. And after being alone for what felt like years now, I remembered that I hated cooking alone. True Love and I used to cook together while we played music. And he'd even let me play those Christmas Carols that he hated so much. But now the house was silent, and I sat in the kitchen, staring into the fridge, reminding myself that I did this.

The list went on. For days I tallied all the things that he gave me or more so the things I lost in his absence. And I wondered if my stubbornness was worth it. Was not wanting to accept death worth living like this?

On the fifth day of Christmas, my phone rang. It rang again on the sixth, and again on the seventh, the eighth, the ninth, and the tenth. I kept it glued to my side incase True Love were to call and apologize, say he was sorry for leaving me alone like he did. But it was my dad who called. I didn't answer because I didn't want to hear his ghostly voice, didn't want him to scrutinize me for not going to Mom's funeral, didn't want him to beg me to care just a little bit more like True Love did.

On the eleventh day of Christmas, Dad sent me a text message. I didn't have to hear his voice if I was just reading his words. It seemed safer to open the message than it did to answer his calls. If I didn't like what he said, I could just delete it and his haunting voice wouldn't be stuck in my head forever.

"Moved to town. New owners are coming to the house tomorrow. Was there anything in the house you wanted?" he asked.

I was lying in bed as I read the message. It was dark in the room, and I squinted against the bright light of my phone. As the words became blurred from staring at them too long, I did a mental inventory of my parents' house.

My dad had a huge collection of bikes that he hung in the wall of the garage. I used to have a small purple bike hanging there with his. We went on a few bike rides together when I was a kid. We didn't talk much when we rode. We just stopped to feed the ducks and stick our feet in the river. I didn't care about my bike that was still there. I was probably too big for it now anyway.

Then there were the paintings my mom had up in the room that used to be mine. They were all of horses. I did like the one of a white horse she had hanging on the back of the door. I liked the way the horse's mane was braided down the side. As a kid, I used to try and braid my hair that way, only to fail when I realized it wasn't thick enough. But I didn't care enough about the painting to go back and get it now.

There were a few other trinkets I had in mind. I used to have a little doll that sat on the mantle of the fireplace over there. I don't know where I got it, but it stayed there even after I moved out. There was something about the way my mom hated that blonde, messy haired doll that made me love it so much.

Dad kept a pile of my scrapbooks sitting somewhere on a book shelf. I used to look through them alone and remind myself of all the ways I was growing up, all the things I used to do as a kid, things that I didn't do anymore. I didn't care too much about the scrapbooks now. They were just a distant reminder of when I was a naïve girl who didn't know how rough the world really was. I didn't need any more reminders now. And like counting sheep, I fell asleep thinking about all the things I didn't care about anymore.

I woke up in a sweat sometime in the middle of the night. My body was freezing like I'd just been hit by a gust of cold air. As I sat straight up from the mattress that was now drenched in my sweat, I could only think about one thing— Hammer. There was one thing at my parents' house that I didn't want to leave behind.

I jumped out of bed and shoved my feet into my boots without socks. I was in too much of a hurry to worry about small things like that. I didn't even put on a bra as I raced to the living room and looked for my keys under the couch cushions where I heard them fall the night before. I pulled the thickest scarf I had over my neck, the one that still smelled like apple cider, and I ran out the front door, slamming it shut as if this was too important for my neighbors not to hear about.

I don't remember much about the drive except for that I kept looking back to the clock. It was 12:05 in the morning when I finally got on the road. My parents' house was only a few miles away, but the fresh snow that fell onto my windshield in thick sprinkles slowed me down.

When I was finally pulling into my parents' driveway, I had to squint to see clearly through the heavy blanket of snow that fell from the sky. I pulled my face down to protect it from the frozen rain drops as I stepped out of the car. It felt like the ground was being pulled out from beneath me as I slipped on the icy driveway and fell on my back into the lawn.

I wasn't physically hurt from the fall because the pillow of snow cushioned me, but I was falling apart inside. I couldn't do anything to fix it, and I lay in the snow wondering where it all went wrong. But I didn't have to wonder for long because I was convinced it all went wrong when I thought that true love was something I should base all my happiness on.

Eventually, I gathered my pride and sat up from the snow. My body was covered in the white powder, and my toes were already getting numb. I reached into the door of my car for the flashlight before closing it. After I walked through the gate to my parents' backyard, the flashlight showing my path, I stopped and stood in front of my mom's garden. Somewhere beneath those flowers is where my *first* true love was buried.

When I was twenty, I still lived with my parents. True Love and I were looking for a house at the time, but it wasn't something I wanted to rush, so I stayed in the garage while I tried to set up my career. The summer Hammer turned twenty-two there was this design conference out of town. It was a few days long, but I knew that if I went, I could meet other designers who could help me with a project that I'd been developing.

So I left my parents to care for Hammer—just food and water every day for three or four days at most. I knew it wouldn't have been much to ask from a friend, but to my mom, it was like I was selling her my soul.

When I came back home, Hammer was in an urn on the kitchen table. They just sat him there for me to find, with no explanation as to why he was trapped in the metal urn instead of greeting me at the door. The only reason I knew it was him was because of the metal plate on the top of the urn that had his name etched onto it, and the urn was heavy— heavy with my Hammer inside.

"What happened?" I asked as I dropped my bag and held the urn in my hands.

"Oh honey … I'm so sorry. He passed while you were away. I didn't want to bother you at your conference—I knew how important that was to you. So I just took care of him for you. Poor guy just died right in his sleep," my mom said with sorrow although I knew she was secretly happy to be rid of him.

That was it, no call, no text, no, 'dear I'm sorry but you should come home because your true love died'. I wanted to bury Hammer so other dogs would find his bones later like they would mine—the circle of life and all that. But he was just a pile of ash in a shiny urn that felt so cold in my fingers that it hurt.

I was so angry then, angry because she didn't tell me, because I couldn't see him one last time and bury him. I was angry because a part of me couldn't help but wonder if she actually killed him.

I laughed as I thought of how ridiculous it must have looked; me running into the back yard with the urn in my arms, ripping up my mom's flower bed, digging a hole there to put Hammer in the ground where he belonged. And I did it partially to spite her because she loved her flowers more than she loved Hammer, more than I could ever love her.

He was still there now, underneath the dirt and new layer of snow. I buried him right by the fence post that was red instead of brown like the rest. The flashlight was still in my hand as I looked at each post, and I knelt on the ground as I came to the one. I plunged my arm deep into the snow and brushed it away from the flowers. I could feel the stems of most of them snap as if their heads were ripped off with the snow.

Then there was the dirt. I clawed into the earth, my fingers feeling like they were peeling apart as I dug my hand into the frozen dirt. Eventually, I dropped the flashlight and kicked up the dirt with cupped hands like an animal. And I liked to pretend that I was the new owner of the house, exploring through the yard, looking for something that would be fun to talk about at parties.

I'm not sure how long I was digging in the dark like that. And I didn't know how long my fingers could keep working before they snapped like icicles. But eventually … I found him.

The urn felt like a rock at first, but when my hands slid over the smooth curve of the base, I knew this was it. I relied on my fingers as I searched for the top of the urn in the dark. Then I gripped it with both hands, being careful not to twist the top off. I cringed as I thought about what would happen if lid came off, spilling Hammer's dust all over the garden and letting it mix in with the dirt and snow. But I was careful as I unearthed him, and I pulled him upward slowly like a secret that was buried for centuries. I was so exhausted that I just held Hammer to my chest and lay on the ground, letting the snow gather around me.

I thought I was going to be happy that I finally had him again. And I even smiled as my fingers brushed past his name plate that was caked in dirt. Maybe my body was confused, maybe it forgot what happy meant, but I cried. I didn't know why I cried, but it was a cry so heavy that all I could do was wait for it to be over. If the neighbors were listening, they might have thought the yard was haunted because my cries sounded ghostly just like my dad's did.

I was so unsure about all that was happening with my body then, why my chest quaked in the absence of breath, the breath that my sobs stole. I didn't know why I cried, but I knew it wasn't because of Hammer.

I cried because of the dirt, because of the iridescent flower petals that were tangled in my hair with the chunks of white snow. I cried because of the heavy urn in my arms, not because of what was in it, but because it existed in all its sturdiness. It kept Hammer safe. After years of being in the ground, he was still there. I cried because he was still there. I cried because my mom actually cared a little bit, enough to keep him there. And I cried because I never got to know that part of her. It was too late to know that part of her.

I looked up at the beam the flashlight left on the frosted grass, and I saw one powder blue flower that remained intact. That flower was my mom. I understood now why True Love left. It didn't matter that Mom and I didn't get along and never would have. She was still a person. She was a person who loved flowers, loved horses, loved to hear the sound of her own voice. She was still a person who craved my attention even if she didn't deserve it. She was a person who cared enough to make sure that Hammer was safe even after he died. I cried again because I thought once she could have killed Hammer. I cried because I knew that could never be true. And I cried because I didn't get to see the 'person' her and not the 'mom' her one last time. I cried because I didn't know where she was buried.

Eventually, the crying stopped. And I'm not big on epiphanies, but I thanked the stupid, torn up garden for reminding me what was important. True Love would have been proud. Before digging myself out of the pile of snow and dirt around me, I reach over and grabbed the blue flower, clutching the stem between my fingers. It was the only surviving flower of my destruction, and I did all I could to keep it safe.

Hammer sat in the front seat of the car with the flower while I drove home. Dirt and snow masked the seats, something I'm sure True Love would have cared about, but I didn't. I waited for my tears to dry as I listened to *Jingle Bells* play on the radio. And I felt bitter because my Christmas and New Year had been glazed over when I fell into a pit of apathy. But I knew as I walked to my front door, that there would always be another year.

I nearly dropped the urn as I opened the door and saw him standing by the fire place. He was wearing the sweater I made for him that had *'Rex'* printed on the front. And he looked so different because he had combed his hair, shaved his face, and he didn't have any cold sores.

"Oh … you're back," I said as I took my shoes off at the door and shook the dirt off of them.

"Is that okay?" he asked as he lingered near the small fire that grew and danced around the new logs.

I nodded as I walked to the kitchen and sat Hammer's urn on the counter. My heart was playing games in my chest because I didn't know if he was home to stay, or if he was just back to get the rest of his things. So I went to the sink and filled a vase up with water and let the stem of the flower fall into it. His eyes were glued on me as I walked into the living room and sat the vase with the flower on the coffee table.

"A flower?" he asked as he pointed to the vase.

I sighed as I felt the tears well again, could feel my throat tighten like my body was telling me not to speak.

"It's Mom," I said as my voice wavered and my face grew warm.

I wasn't sure what was going to happen after that. I hadn't planned for any of it to happen. I was just hoping that if he was going to leave, he'd stay for a little bit longer.

"You look awful," he said as he walked to me and suddenly wrapped me in his arms.

I was shocked, but my stomach grew warm as I heard Stan come down the hall and felt him rub against my leg. I wanted to fight it. I didn't want to believe that this was real because it all seemed too good. I didn't want to forget that I was miserable not long ago. I was afraid to accept the smile that threatened to show on my lips as I inhaled the scent of his cologne.

"I'm sorry I left like that …" he said as he kept holding onto me, as if I would disappear if he let go.

"I'm sorry I let you go," I said through ragged breaths, feeling the warm tears hit my cheeks.

"It was stupid. After your mom, I just didn't think you cared. I was just afraid you didn't know what was important … that if I … well … I wasn't sure if you thought I was important," he admitted.

"I know what's important now," I said as I crumpled his sweater in my hands and held him close.

On the first day of Christmas, my true love gave to me cold sores and crippling depression. On the last day, he gave me hope.

Unknown Blessing | *Krystle Kwiatkowski*

Friendships are rough.

The dynamic unique

in each one.

Some feel like the Leader,

Others feel like the Baggage.

No matter the role, though,

be wary to take it for granted …

My hands trembled as I received what was left of my money: Four dollars and seventeen cents. I refused to worry too much about it since what little shopping I was given money to do is done. Well, all except getting my dad something. But I knew he would understand. I gave a half-smile to the lady who gave me my change and pocketed the money.

"Thank you," I said softly, as I took my tray of food down the rows of tables in the chaotic mall. I spied an empty table and went to sit down, only to land in something wet.

I rose to my feet and glanced at the seat, now smeared in ketchup.

Great. There goes my good pair of jeans.

I stabbed the sesame chicken with my plastic fork and lifted it to my mouth, wincing as the book suddenly bopped me over the head. Keeping my gaze straight-forward, I watched Chloe sit down to the right of me. I noticed her black, almost shoulder length hair was exactly the same as when we arrived at the mall. I guessed she didn't have enough leftover money to get her hair done like she wanted.

Rolling my eyes, I proceeded to eat my Chinese food. After the first couple bites of the chicken, I realized I had forgotten to get some soy sauce to go with my white rice. I glanced back for a moment, studying the crowd before shrugging it off. There was no way I was walking back through that chaos again.

Despite how much I loved the holiday, the worst part was always the chaos that grew more and more until the final days of Christmas. And the final days were here. The mall would be closing in three, four hours tops. That was the normal closing time for most stores two days before Christmas.

"Nick," I heard Edgar's voice say as he sat across from me. He waved his brown hair out of his eyes. "Did you ever get that thing for your dad?"

"I didn't have enough money," I grumbled.

He narrowed his eyes as he glanced at the bag next to me. "But you had the fifty bucks to buy that video game."

I swallowed as I felt the heat rising in me. I wished people would mind their own business. "Shut up," I said quietly. "I've been wanting this game forever."

He silently stared back at me with his bright blue eyes, clearly annoyed. Rolling his eyes, his blonde girlfriend Hailey came and stood beside him. She kneeled a little to kiss Edgar before sitting down.

"PDA," I said, annoyed.

Edgar looked back at me. "Sorry—"

"Then stop rubbing it in!" I snapped with a raised voice.

"We're—we're not," Hailey mumbled.

"That's all y'all ever do. And you," I pointed at Zack, who had just sat down at the table.

A hand was placed on my shoulder. "Calm down," Chloe said.

"I am calm!" I shouted again. I looked back at Edgar. "You know, it's funny. You wouldn't even be dating her if she wasn't a cheerleader and—and if she wasn't such a gorgeous blondie—"

"Excuse me?" Edgar gasped, taken by surprise.

"All you are is a pretty little face," I said, glaring at Hailey. "That's all you've ever been."

Hailey immediately stood to her feet, showing only a small hint of fury in her face. She was an expert at hiding her feelings. Not taking her eyes off me, she said, "I'm not going to listen to this prick."

"Hailey, wait—" Edgar said, but she already stormed off. He turned back to me. "You just don't know how to keep your mouth shut, do you?"

"Oh, you know it's true!"

Edgar glared at me, furious. "When are you going to learn to grow up? I thought we were friends. But right now you're treating everyone like dirt."

"Maybe I wish we had never become friends," I snapped, standing to my feet. I glanced down at my food, my appetite gone. I looked back at him. "Now you know what it's like to be treated like nothing."

I grabbed my bag and left my food, in a hurry to get outside. I had never been so angry before. At least not at Edgar. I've done so many things for him, been there for him when he needed me. And this is what I got in return. But not anymore. I'm tired of being treated like I'm invisible. I was sick of being under-appreciated.

The automatic doors opened before me and the frosty air hit me. But it wasn't nearly cold enough to cool me down. Plus, it was East Texas. We rarely get freezing temperatures or snow during Winter.

I took a step through the walking lane and flinched when a car honked at me. After the car passed, I gave them the bird and proceeded to race down the sidewalk to my dad's truck, which he let me borrow. I began gasping for air and closed my eyes for several seconds before shifting the truck in gear and pulling out of the parking lot.

As I approach the first red light, I thought back to what I said. For some reason I was asking myself twice if I had any regrets. But no. I really did wish Edgar and I had never became friends. Life would be a hell of a lot better. Not just for me, but for them too. Sometimes I really did need to keep my mouth shut, but I was too proud to admit it.

I realized I zoned out and deep in thought as the car behind me honked. I jumped in my seat and shifted the truck into first gear. As I approached the next light, I sped up just as it turned green. I drove through the green signal light while the cars in the next lane slowed down, and a horn suddenly sounded to the right of me.

I had no time to dodge the incoming semi-truck. Headlights blinding me, I felt the truck flip to the side as everything went black.

* * *

My eyes opened immediately, and I found myself in my bed. Weird, I thought. That was easily the weirdest dream I ever had. Glancing at my phone, I notice the date.

December 19th, the last day of school before Christmas break. And yet I could have sworn it was two days before Christmas. But then, my dream must have had me really confused. I stared at my phone blinking, watching the date staying the same before noticing the time. I really needed to get to school if I wanted to meet my friends before the first bell.

It didn't take long for me to get ready. I just grabbed a random black t-shirt from my closet and pulled on the same pair of jeans I'd been wearing all week. I sniffed under my arm and shrugged as I left the house. Luckily, I lived half a mile from the school and it was easily a quick walk as long as I didn't take my time.

Once I made it to the cafeteria, I walked through the doors and headed to our normal spot. But the round table was empty, so I suspected that the others were running a bit late. Instead of leaving, I took a seat and waited for them.

Fifteen minutes passed and none of my friends had arrived yet. It wasn't normal that they were all late, but I decided it was best to just head to class. I still had ten minutes until the first bell.

I grabbed whatever books I needed and closed my locker. From the corner of my eye I saw James heading towards me. I turned the other way and heard him shouting my name. Sneaking in an empty classroom, I waited for him to pass. I saw him go by without noticing me and left the room, going the other way. But I wanted to be sure. I glanced behind me to make sure James didn't see me—

"Watch it, wimp!" a familiar voice scowled.

I turned and faced Zack, smiling. Cody was also with him. "Hey, man—"

"Don't you 'hey, man,' me," he shouted offensively, knocking the books out of my hands. Giving Cody the fist bump, they shoved me against the lockers and left, laughing as if it was fun.

What was wrong with him? Zack and I were always close, ever since I'd known him. Sure, he'd always pick on me, but not like that.

As they rounded the corner, I noticed James coming back. "Dude," he said, stepping beside me, patting my shoulder. "Didn't you hear me call you? You just took off like a bat out of hell. Are we still hanging out after school?"

I was suddenly too terrified to move. I barely moved my eyes just enough to study his face. *James and I are … friends? And Zack … wait, why was—hold on. They've gotta be playing some kind of trick on me.* James was the bully, not my friend Zack. Yet I could see it in his eyes. He wasn't joking.

"I'll … have to get back to you on that," I said, walking off.

"At lunch, then!" he shouted.

Rounding the corner, I was desperate to find Edgar. He would know what was going on. Suddenly, I bumped into Chloe, and I was happy to see another familiar face. Hailey stood next to her, and suddenly, I'm not quite sure what I said to her was in a dream or not.

"Hey, um," I looked at Hailey, "first off, I'm really sorry for what I said the other day. I didn't mean it. I was just aggravated and—"

"What are you talking about?" Hailey answered, chewing gum as she grimaced.

How could she had forgotten? "The thing I said, I didn't mean it."

"We haven't spoken in forever," she said. "In fact, we never do."

Shaking my head, I couldn't believe what I was hearing. "Maybe Edgar will know what's going on here. Chloe," I asked her, "do you know where he is? I haven't seen him all morning. I really need to talk to him."

Chloe stared back at me with her dark eyes. For a moment she was completely expressionless as if she saw a ghost, and then she was suddenly holding back the tears and storming away.

"Chloe, wait!" I tried to go after her, but an arm blocked my path.

"What the hell is wrong with you?" Hailey questioned. She didn't even give me a chance to answer as she went to follow Chloe and comfort her.

First Zack and James. Now Chloe. "Why is everyone acting so weird?" I said out loud.

"Because you were never there," another familiar voice chimed in.

Please, let it be somebody who can help me. I turned and looked up at the face of Drake Arkana. "Holy … Drake! What are you doing h—no—do you know what is going on? Everyone is acting weird!"

"You got your wish," he said casually. He wrapped his arm across my shoulder as he led me down the hall. "You and Edgar were never friends."

"I don't—but that was a dream, wasn't it?"

"Was it?"

I took a deep breath and exhaled loudly. "I don't get it. What would be the big deal, anyways? Zack and I are—or were friends. James is—or was—dang it, I don't even know! And despite Cody and I never liking each other, even he never acts like this!"

"You threw away your friendship like it was nothing," Drake replied. "And for that, this is your new reality."

"But I was just tired of being under-appreciated."

"That's not what friendship is even about. It's about always being there for one another, even when you think you're invisible." He sighed and took his arm off me, looking straight at me. "Nick, it's okay to feel under-appreciated sometimes. But is it really worth throwing away a friendship for?"

I let out another deep breath. "Well, maybe at least now I won't be in the way anymore. I was always in the way of my friends' happiness. Always making bad jokes at the wrong times."

Drake looked at me with a blank face. "Happy? Maybe you should take yet another look at what you really wished for. But to understand the present, you have to dive into the past."

Rolling my eyes, a swirling, dark purple vortex appeared in front of me. I glanced back at Drake and shook my head. "I am not going in there. There's nothing I need to see."

"You have no choice."

"The Drake I knew wouldn't force me—"

"Today I am not the Drake you knew. Today I am an archangel. The Archangel of Christmas Past."

I let out a slight laugh and rolled my eyes. "I told you, I'm not—"

He pushed me before I had a chance to finish, and suddenly I was falling backwards as the darkness overtook me. But then, I found myself standing on a familiar street, watching two people.

"That's me," I said out loud. "And Zack."

"You remember?"

I didn't even realize Drake was standing beside me. Of course he would stick around.

"I'm not sure," I answered, watching my younger self pushing Zack with a laugh.

Zack pushed him back, warning him, "Watch it."

"Don't push me," young-Nick said. He pushed Zack yet again, laughing.

"You started it," Zack elbowed him in the side, pushing the other me a few feet into the road. Sometimes Zack didn't know his own strength.

"We were in fifth grade," I realized as a cark honked its horn, followed by the sound of screeching brakes. But Zack tackled the younger me as the car hit him instead.

"Zack saved my life that day," I continued. "All my friends thought I was the one who walked into the road without paying attention. But it was Zack. And he felt responsible. Even though I was the one that started all the horse-playing."

"He saved you because that's the kind of heart he had," Drake intervened.

I looked at him. "Had?" I questioned, but he only gestured back to the scene.

A man got out of the car to check on Zack, pulling out his phone to call an ambulance. As I watched the younger me walking over to check on him, the scene dissolved like it never happened. Then, I saw Zack walking down the sidewalk alone. Seconds later, that same car drove by.

"Wait, what happened?" I asked.

Drake shook his head. "That's the thing. It never happened."

"But it just—" I tried to say, but Drake interrupted once again.

"Don't you remember how you and Zack met?"

"Yeah, we were first introduced by Ed—oh."

Drake nodded. "Without you," he began, pointing at the spot where the car previously hit my friend, "this day never happened. Zack never had the accident, never got put in a wheelchair. Never grown to respect people the way he did."

"And now he's the school bully," I said. I now realized what an idiot I was and wondered if this was the most damage that I caused. It had to be. "And Cody? Why is he a bully with Zack?"

"Because you and Cody always hated each other. The more bad things you said about Cody, the more he came to respect Edgar. You actually brought them closer together."

"Then how did me and James become so close? Wouldn't he be right alongside them?"

"There can only be one leader. Zack took that spot. James was downplayed and eventually became a loser. Like you."

Glaring at Drake, I said, "Watch it." He seriously had no idea how mad I could get.

Drake snapped his fingers and another portal appeared. Looking back at me, he said, "You know the drill."

I scoffed at him. "Let's just get this over with." I leapt through, unsure of what to expect next. At least it couldn't be worse than James and Zack switching spots in who ran the school.

The smell of soft grass hit me as a wind breezed through the air. Grayish pillars of stone were neatly organized throughout the green field, surrounded by a fence—

Turning to face Drake, I scoffed yet again. "A graveyard? Really? What the hell are we doing here?"

He remained silent as he focused his gaze behind me. Spinning on my feet, I saw Chloe kneeling at a grave, Edgar standing next to her.

"Dude," I said, "there you are." But he didn't seem to notice me. "Dude!" I walk over to him, then notice that Chloe was kneeling before her father's grave. I suddenly remembered that she visited her father often, usually with

Edgar by her side. "Sorry," I said, realizing why he was ignoring me. "But I tried finding you at school. I need to talk to—"

Upon brushing my elbow against him, I noticed his transparent figure as my arm went through him. Glaring at Drake, I spread my arms in the air. "Really?"

"To understand the present—"

"Oh, shut up, Drake." I turned back to my friends and muttered, "Archangel of Christmas punks …"

Edgar placed his hand on Chloe's shoulder to comfort her. It was obvious that he knew his boundaries. Not too close, but not too far. He stayed in that gray area of friend zone.

She stood to her feet and turned to face me. Or turned to face Edgar, since I wasn't technically there. Neither of them knew that. Chloe hugged Edgar and laid her head on his shoulder for a moment before they both became transparent.

"Oh come on," I said. "Even if I wasn't in the picture, Edgar would still be here by Chloe's side comforting her. Right?" I turned back to face Drake, but he was gone. "Drake? Where did—"

I finally noticed Chloe's transparent figure appear a few rows down, on her knees before another grave. This time, she had fresh tears in her eyes.

"I'm sorry I couldn't protect you," she said. "I failed you."

As I approached, I realized that Chloe was hurting. Like, really hurting. I had never seen her so broken like that before, even when the subject of her father was brought up.

"He should have taken me with you. Yeah, that would have been better. More peaceful. All this guilt and pain I'm feeling, and you not by my side. I need my best friend. I need you. Eddie, I'm sorry I wasn't stronger."

My face grew stiff as I lifted my head. What did she just say? I wanted to move around the grave to get a clear view, but I was suddenly dizzy, my heart about to beat out of my chest. I hobbled around and read: 'Rest In Peace: Edgar Joseph Freeman. August 24th 1992—August 24th 2007.'

"No … " I gasped, as I read the name over and over again, glancing back at Chloe's broken figure kneeling at the grave. "No! No-no-no-no-no! NO!!" Adrenaline rushed through me as I became completely unfocused. I looked around for Drake once again, but he's still nowhere to be found. "Drake! You get your ass back here right now! You have some explaining to do!"

"What is there to explain?" his voice suddenly echoed in the air.

He was still nowhere to be seen. "This is all your fault, Drake. You take me back to where I belong right now!"

"But this is what you wanted, is it not?"

"No!" I shouted, frustrated now.

"This is what you wished for."

"Don't you *dare* pin this on me! I did not ask for anyone to die! And especially not—" I collapsed on the grass.

"Not Edgar. Not my best friend." Tears slid down the side of my cheeks and I didn't care to wipe them away.

I jumped to my feet as a hand touched my shoulder. Looking into the eyes of Drake once again, I pushed him away. Then, I used my powers and shot a massive ball of fire at him.

But it just went straight through him. Of course.

Pointing at Drake, my hands shook as I growled. "Fix. This. Now!"

"Things can only be changed or fixed through responsibility."

"You're saying I have to claim responsibility for whatever happened to Edgar? Never! I never asked for this!"

"Where were you the day of Edgar's fifteenth birthday? The day that you all received powers? Or the day King Henry came to your school disguised as someone else?"

I knew the answer, but I also knew that it wasn't going to be correct. The answer was that I wasn't there. Not if Edgar and I weren't friends. But why was this such a big deal?

Drake sighed. "You still don't understand do you?"

"I—" I struggled to find the words, but I just couldn't.

"You were the glue in that friendship. The one that made all the difference. Without you, there is no group."

Another portal opened before me. Already I was dreading it. But I desperately needed to know the answer now. What did I do that was so bad that Edgar wouldn't be here today? Despite how bad I wanted to know, I shook nervously as I entered. I hoped this was the last thing Drake would show me. I had no idea how much more of this I could bare.

A familiar sight came into view as woods grew around me. Edgar was on his knees, as was Zack and the two blonde girls, Crystal and Jordan. Just a few months ago we were all here fighting King Henry. It was only a few months ago when the rest of my friends were at King Henry's mercy, as his five Dark Warriors stood beside him. But this evil king had no mercy.

I glanced over to where my past self had just arrived with James, right after I had convinced him to help us. Any moment now we would be jumping out to distract the bad guys. Any moment now we would be saving the day—

"Let me fix that," Drake said, whispering in my ear as if he knew what I was thinking.

Gasping, I realized exactly what was going to happen. I looked over at myself hiding behind a tree, waiting to pop out. The younger me faded, followed by James. Glancing back at the rest of my friends, I watched them fade one by one, as if they were never there. Eventually, it was just Edgar left, despite Chloe being added to the group.

"Where did Crystal and Jordan go?" I asked. "Are you saying I killed them too? And why is Chloe here?"

"King Henry always knew who Edgar was without you being there to divert his attention. He killed those two girls when they were watching Edgar's house, waiting for Henry to attack. They were caught off guard. And with everything happening sooner than planned, Henry never made that virus that possessed Edgar's friend, Chloe. This is the recipe for disaster that you have created."

Everything Drake said made perfect sense to me, as the final pieces of the puzzles mended itself together.

"I figured you would want this," one of the Dark Warriors said as he approached King Henry. He lifted a sword, flashing it in his face.

King Henry unsheathed the sword with one hand and turned to Edgar. Tears fell from Chloe's face as she begged for mercy, as she begged for Henry to kill her and spare him.

"Girl, shut up!" King Henry bellowed.

"No …" I groaned. "Please …" I dashed forward to tackle the evil king, desperate to save Edgar. Instead, I went through him like a ghost.

"What's done has already been done," Drake said. "There is no turning back. You cannot change the damage that has been done."

"No!" I shouted. "There has to be another way! I can fix this!" I tackled Henry again, determined to break the butterfly effect that I created. "Please!" I yelled, hitting the ground once again.

King Henry raised his sword beside Edgar's neck. "Any last words … boy?"

Edgar only glared back at him. Then, he appeared to be clearing his throat to speak but instead, he spat in Henry's face.

"Hmm. Brave," he said.

"Please, Drake," I begged. "Don't let this happen, do something! Please, no, I don't want to see this!"

King Henry raised his sword, and swung it so fast that it pierced the very air. I turned my gaze a different direction as the sword took off Edgar's head.

I couldn't bear to look at the leftover scene. I could only lay on the ground like a wounded animal, hoping and wishing and praying for a second chance.

"I'm—I'm sorry, Edgar. I took our friendship for g— for granted just for a little appreciation." The tears continuously streamed out of my eyes as I succumbed to the darkness, accepting responsibility for all I had done.

I wasn't there. I deserved this. Edgar didn't.

I wished I had a second chance to be a better friend. No recognition in the world was worth any of this.

Suddenly, I was falling, shouting at the top of my lungs when someone caught me. Upon opening my eyes, my breath was taken away as I looked up at Chloe's worried face.

"It was a nightmare," she said in a worrisome voice.

Shock took the words out of my mouth as I glanced around a white room, a wooden door directly to my left.

"Am I…in the hospital?" I asked, suddenly confused.

"Yeah, you …" Chloe's voice trailed off as she sighed. "You had a wreck. Some idiot ran a red light. Luckily, you're healing faster than a normal person would. But nothing major other than a broken arm."

So it *was* a dream.

"You almost rolled off the bed after randomly muttering Edgar's name," she continued.

I looked at her. "Edgar?" I asked as adrenaline rushed through me. "Is Edgar all right?"

"He's fine," she said, suddenly confused. "He's right there."

I veered my head to the opposite side of the bed. Edgar had his head on the bed obviously asleep.

A rush of relief like I could never describe flooded through me. "How long has he been there?"

"Since your wreck," Chloe said, biting her lip. "Which was two days ago. Edgar got here as soon as he heard. And … he hasn't left since."

I felt my face turn red from guilt as I looked back at him. Edgar was always there for everyone. And now, he was here for me. And after I treated him like dirt.

"You're okay," I said to her.

Lines appeared in her face as she opened her mouth to speak. Then, she tilted her head while squinting her eyes. "Was that a question?"

Giving a half smile, I shook my head. "Never mind." It was all okay after all.

Edgar began muttering nonsense as he rubbed the top of his head. Lifting his head off the bed, his face went from sleepy to wide awake and alert in less than a second.

"Nick," he gasped. "Are you okay?"

I felt guilty that he was worried about me. I was more worried about him. "I'm … *so* sorry for what I said. I didn't mean it—but—I mean, I have no excuse for what I said. I was angry and—"

"No, it's okay, man," Edgar said. "We all have our moments."

"Not like this…" I muttered as someone entered the room.

But it wasn't just someone. It was everyone. Zack, Cody, and even Hailey.

"Hailey," I began to say, but she cut me off.

"You don't need to explain yourself. You got heated. I get it. I know you're not that kind of person. And Edgar thinks highly of you, so …"

Suddenly I realized the silent appreciation that was happening here. When I was around, I felt under-appreciated. But when I wasn't, it was so much more. Edgar obviously cared more than I ever thought.

Hailey put an arm around Edgar as she approached him. "Merry Christmas," she said.

My eyes widened. "Wait, today is Christmas? Why aren't you all at home?"

"Because Edgar refused to leave," Hailey said. "And … truth is, we all agreed to come up here and be with you. All of us. Together."

I was completely overwhelmed. They wanted all of us to be together. Even me. "You didn't have to do that."

Edgar glared at me. "Of course we did. We wouldn't leave you out. It's not the same without you."

"You have no idea," I whispered. "Also, is there any way one of you can take me back to the mall tomorrow? I should return that stupid game and get my father something."

"Whoa," Zack said, surprised. "What's gotten into you? Nicky-boy returning a videogame? Were you probed while you were unconscious?"

The old Zack was definitely back. And here I was, laying in a hospital bed and being picked on already. "Oh, haha," I said. "It's just, there are so many things I could be doing to show my appreciation for people instead of wasting money on games all the time."

My friends smiled at my words, and it also surprised me how much I meant what I said. And from now on, I was going to start treating them different. I mean, I guess I would still make jokes. Things wouldn't be the same without them. And I'm freaking hilarious.

"Merry Christmas, guys," I said. "I love you all and wouldn't trade you for the world."

They all smiled back at me.

"Friendship is everything." They would never know what I meant by that.

And that was okay.

Always, But Not Forever | *Chelsea Lauren*

Sometimes soulmates aren't

forever mates.

Often, we are led

down different paths.

Neither more right

nor more wrong.

But the existence,

the feelings,

the conversations,

and experiences shared

can never be broken.

A bond unspoken.

Happy EX-Mas | *Chelsea Lauren*

The house was silent, but the smell of coffee and warm cinnamon buns seeped its way under the door. We had chosen to pretend things were the same—one last time.

Aside from the fact that, I well … I was waking up in our guest bedroom—one I had temporarily been banished to for the past five days.

No one knew. We were both in denial, I think. Maybe, maybe if we had just one last perfect Christmas, my mind would suddenly change, and we could pretend it was like nothing ever happened.

We were fooling ourselves.

As I crept down the stairs, he was curled on the couch in his brand-new pajama's. We always purchased each other new pajama's and got to open them every Christmas Eve. Yesterday was no different, aside from the awkward silences and mumbled 'thank you's.'

I didn't have the courage to wear mine last night, not that I often wore pajamas to bed, but I had the last week. Something felt strange about sleeping naked—even if it was my own home. But I had put the pajamas on before I went downstairs, grateful he had chosen to do the same.

There was a cup of coffee and a cinnamon bun on the coffee table for me. And his was there right next to my own, getting cold.

We never waited.

Rounding the corner of the couch, I took a seat on the far end, giving an entire cushion between us.

"Merry Christmas," I said softly.

His Adam's apple bobbed, and he blinked a few times before looking over my way.

"Merry Christmas."

Carter's eyes were rimmed red and bloodshot, yet there was effort in his appearance. His face was clean-shaven and his often unruly bed head was brushed into place as it dried. Those were the only things he could control though. The bags under his eyes darkened each day and I feared the creases in his forehead would forever be permanent.

I felt inadequate sitting next to him. He was trying his hardest to impress me, woo me back to him. And here I sat, going on two days of not showering—my greasy hair matted to my scalp—hoping I had the energy to pursue the next few hours.

This was a stupid idea, I shouldn't have suggested this. Looking over at the tree, there was an abundance of presents for our family and friends.

This year we had made the decision that we would be spending Christmas in our new town. Well, I shouldn't say new. We've lived here for almost two years now. The first year, we went home as often as we could both get off of work. This year, we made the promise to really establish ourselves and who we were as a couple. This meant we went home for Thanksgiving, but we decided we'd start our own Christmas traditions—and our families decided they were going to come visit us this year—we'd host Christmas around New Year's.

We hadn't discussed how this would pan out.

We may both not survive another five days.

"Thank you for breakfast."

"Of course." He was also staring straight ahead at the tree.

In the past, ever since we started living with each other five years ago, I would make the coffee and he would make the cinnamon buns. I'd always overlook the process, adding more icing than he cared for—this year, mine had just the right amount of icing.

I took it upon myself to begin eating because honestly, who wants a cold cinnamon bun? At least this way I could think of ways to start today.

He followed suit and we both silently ate—staring blindly at the fresh Christmas tree and the pine needle collection on the ground.

It was always Carter's idea to get a fresh tree and he was responsible for the clean up too, that was the deal. But, I guess that was the least of our worries.

My mouth was about to utter a pet name, muscle memory of having spoken so many pet names over the course of our twelve year relationship.

"Carter?" The last bite of my cinnamon roll lodged itself in my esophagus. He didn't respond, but I did get him to look over at me. I'll take that as more of a win. "Are we making a mistake here?"

The way his eyes turned to stone just twisted the knife further into my stomach.

"In what regard are you talking about?"

I shouldn't have eaten breakfast. If he wasn't careful, I'd be spewing cinnamon roll all over our carpet.

Our … was anything even mine anymore?

"Spending Christmas together."

His lips pursed together as he gave a curt nod. He was hoping for a different answer, but I couldn't give that to him. Shouldn't he be able to understand that?

"Aidan," he sighed.

I bit my lip and swallowed continuously until the onset of tears subsided. He hadn't called me Aidan in sixteen years. A.J.? Yes. Any pet name under the sun? Yes. But *never* Aidan.

I caught the scrunch of his nose as my name left a bad taste in his mouth.

"I am trying here. I … I don't know what you want from me."

Carter and I met in preschool, and second grade was the last time he ever called me Aidan. I remember the day clearly—he announced us superhero's because we were A.J. and C.J., ready to take on the world. While my nickname continued, I left C.J. for his other friends to use.

We were instant best friends. We shared almost everything. The two of us were just extensions of both families. When someone asked us how many siblings we had, we answered five. Carter had three siblings and I had two. We never included ourselves in those numbers because that'd just be weird. Carter was the oldest, which is why it has been hard to create our own Christmas. His youngest sister was just going into high school. Whereas for myself, I fell directly in the middle. My oldest sister just turned thirty and my baby brother just turned twenty-one.

We rarely ever spent time apart. The two of us even went on family vacations with the other. It wasn't until we started dating the summer before high school that things started to get more strict with our families. Suddenly, we had rules and sleepovers were little to none. But that didn't keep us from being together all the time.

Naturally, we attended the same college and while we chose to dorm separately for space and to meet new people, we never dated anyone else.

That was the thing, we never dated anyone else, and I was starting to suffocate.

We had our own careers and our own friends—despite a few that have known us forever. We had our own lives, but while we did, they still intermingled.

Especially when going home for holidays, meant going home to the exact same town and same childhood homes.

I was desperate for a change.

But more so, I was desperate to come clean.

We were avoiding the conversation over whether or not we could still be friends. After twenty-three years of friendship, I couldn't imagine going through my life without him. Which is why it took me forever to have this conversation. This wasn't a whim decision. This didn't go down as *I* planned, but unfortunately it happened exactly as planned.

"I'm not upset with how you identify," he said. "I would never," he was staring at me directly now, turning on the couch, "be disappointed in that or not accept you. It's more so, how you went about telling me, or lack thereof."

If my eyes weren't bloodshot from lack of sleep the past few days, they were now. I was the ultimate disappointment and there wasn't a thing I could do to take it back. I knew that now. My mind had righted itself in this moment.

"I'm sorry if I ever gave you reason to believe that we couldn't have this conversation. I thought we told each other everything?" My vision grew cloudy and I dared myself not to look over at him. I'd break. I didn't deserve to be the one in pain here.

"We do. We did." I sighed. "I … that was it. My only secret."

The laugh he let out made my lungs deflate.

"Pretty damn big secret."

I nodded. I couldn't argue with that. I couldn't argue with anything.

"Why?" His voice cracked and I felt the cushions move. He was interlacing our fingers and brought them to his lap as he kneeled on the middle cushion. "Why did it have to be that way?"

He was speaking on behalf of walking in on me sleeping with someone else. It was an affair that had been happening for a month. I had been pulling away and he wasn't an idiot to not notice. I played it off as a slump we were in— I mean, we had been together for so long. Never though … never did the affair take place in our home until a week ago, right about the time when I knew he'd be home from work.

I had been spiraling downward for months—years even—before I first cheated. And then I did it to pity myself and it worked. This was the ultimate fuck you—to both of us.

I didn't know why I was so afraid to ask Carter for space. It wasn't like he was controlling or demanding. It wasn't like he would have hurt me if I said I needed time to think. He was *too* understanding. *Too* loving. I didn't think I deserved the love he'd pour over me with my confession—well the secret before knowing I cheated. So I did what I thought I deserved. If Carter walked in on me in the act, he'd have no other way to react than pure anger.

Unfortunately, that didn't work either.

There wasn't a big explosion. It wasn't some messy scene. He opened the guest bedroom door (I wouldn't be stupid enough to have an affair in our bed) and the look of disgust on his face was enough to shatter my entire being. But then he walked away.

Silence kills.

I shrugged at his question.

"No," his voice demanded now and he jerked my hand to cause me to look at him.

We've barely spoken to each other all week. I had been dreading Christmas the moment I suggested this.

"We are having this conversation if it kills us. Talk to me. You've already done the fucking damage, the least you can do is let me into your head."

Tears were mixing into my coffee mug and soaking the knees of my flannel pants. He took the coffee out of my hand, and placed both of our mugs on the table.

"A.J.," his voice was a whisper. Looking over at him I saw his own cheeks were stained with tears. "We made the decision in kindergarten that we would never not be friends. We had the conversation in high school that we'd never let this ruin our friendship. Ever. I don't want to lose you. I know this isn't you. But I can't see any other way of handling this if you can't open up to me."

I didn't break my eye contact with him. I wanted to be honest. I wanted to tell him about the thoughts poisoning my brain. But I wasn't sure that it would make things better.

He opened his arms and pulled me into them. The knife twisted so deep in the pit of my stomach that I tried to swallow the guilt while growing lightheaded. He was the best friend anyone could ever ask for. He didn't hate me. But he was disappointed in me and honestly, I wasn't sure what was worse.

Carter rested his head on top of mine, hugging me tightly against him. I could hear his rapid heartbeat. He wasn't comfortable, but this is what he did. He solved things. Always. He hated not knowing how to fix something.

There were times throughout our friendship, mainly in college, where I'd get myself into such a panic over stress and the only fix for it was his crushing hugs, keeping me focused and steady.

I loved him for trying right in this moment.

Scratch that, I *did* love him. I *do* love him. If I'm being honest, I don't know if I want to end this. But I need to do this for the both of us, so we can genuinely know if this is best.

I curled into him and he pulled us back so we were laying down on the couch. It would be normal, a normal cuddle on the couch if we weren't both crying. If we both didn't have a death grip on each other because what would happen when we let go?

I could feel his heaving. I could hear his breathing in and out, trying to steady himself—trying to regulate his breath like he's learned in his damn yoga classes. He was trying to be quiet, trying to bring me into a comfort as well.

When he caught me, and I had sent my guest home, we both awkwardly sat at the kitchen table. He had poured himself a scotch and poured me a glass of wine. We were silent for quite some time. I obviously wasn't going to admit to what he saw. I was stubborn. He knew that. But I think he was more confused by who I had an affair with than the fact that I had an affair.

Eventually I had told him that I was almost certain I was bisexual and that I wanted space to find out for sure. He took this as me just wanting to sleep around. Took it internally, thinking he had done something wrong—even pressured me into being gay. That wasn't the case, even if he was the one who convinced me to try us out when we were fourteen. But we didn't discuss how long I had these feelings and why I never spoke of them.

It was mostly because he was being stubborn and close-minded. It couldn't be a conversation about my sexuality because he wasn't ready for it—even if I was.

"How long?" I could feel his breath tickling the back of my neck.

I pulled his hands up from my stomach, bringing them into my chest. I kissed them.

"I don't think I've never not known. I never had a word for it. But I never thought anything about it. I was able to have conversations with you and understand what you were going through, but also have conversations with our other friends. It was the best of both worlds that I never thought I had to identify nor did I really know what that meant. I wasn't ready to date, even when we started to, but then we did and I thought I'd be fine because I loved you. I do love you, Carter. Don't lose sight of that. I never thought it'd come to haunt me, because if I was happy, did it matter?"

"So you're not happy? Is there something I can do?"

The problem with his question was that there were many different layers.

Was I happy in general? No.

Was I happy with him currently? No.

Could he do anything in either situation? No.

I turned in his arms, my eyes readjusting to the little space between us.

"I'm not happy," I sighed. "I haven't been happy for a while but," I paused, pressing a finger to his lips as he was about to speak. "It's not you. It never has been you. Carter?"

I looked into his eyes and I watched the defenses drop as they clouded with more tears. His fingernails dug into my hips.

"I think I need help."

My body deflated in one breath and I was pulled against his chest a second later. His lips were kissing my neck, in between "you're okay," "it's okay," and "it'll all be okay."

"We can get you help. It's okay. Are you depressed? Is it because you've been trying to figure this all out on your own? Love, why couldn't you ever come to me?"

My shoulders trembled and his hands moved to grip them, calming me in place. I didn't have any answers for him.

"I … I need to do this on my own."

He pulled me back so he could take in my face.

"What?"

"Carter, I need to make sure that this is what I really want. I don't know why, but something's happening to me and I can't explain it to you. I'm going from zero to sixty in the matter of seconds and I get these thoughts that I can't control. I'm never happy or satisfied lately and I keep having nightmares of whether this is all enough. I need to go figure out a few things and maybe, maybe I'll end up back here. But maybe you need to go out too."

"No," he shook his head furiously. "No, I don't need to figure it out. You're it for me, Aidan. I don't need to go on some journey to find the one. I thought I was lucky. But I guess I was wrong."

I sat up quick.

"This isn't some stupid journey. This isn't because I don't love you. Fuck, Carter. This is because I *do* love you. I don't want to hurt you. This is killing me just as much as you—possibly even more. But what happens when we're in our fifties and have a family and I start to resent you because

I never had a chance to fully make that decision? Hmm? What then?" My voice rose until I was practically screaming at him.

We rarely screamed.

We rarely fought.

Maybe that was the problem. Maybe we loved each other so much that we were toxic. That we forgave far too many times for things that we should have held our ground on.

"Carter, we're the same goddamn person. Have you ever thought of that? I know everything there is to know about you. It was exciting to meet someone new and learn a whole new world."

"I'm sorry I don't have a brand new life, Aidan! I'm sorry that I'm not interesting enough for you anymore. But fuck, did you have to screw someone in our home?"

I agree that was a mistake. But only because I imagine the night in my head each time I try and sleep on that same damn bed. I think that's causing me to lose more sleep than what's happening between us.

"I didn't know how to tell you."

"So you wanted me to catch you?"

I only nodded. I could tell he was repulsed by me. He didn't want me so close to him. But he was on the inside and I was on the edge of the couch. Carter was too nice to ask me to leave or push me off. So I'd use it to my advantage.

"My brain, it … it convinces me these things are good ideas. It tells me to go down this spiral and I listen because I don't think I deserve anything more. I don't deserve you, that's for sure. I know I should haven't cheated. It was killing me inside each time it happened. But it was the thrill and urge that my brain was telling me this was the only way. I know I need help and I want to get it, Carter. But God, I don't want to lose you as my friend. I need you. I need you here with me. I don't … I don't think I can do it on my own."

I started hyperventilating. The good and the bad were both in my head. There was a turmoil happening and I had no control over either side. The good was winning. The good was trying to defeat the bad. I knew it wouldn't work, but it was enough for me to recognize the actual damage I caused. Enough for me to know that what I did may be irreparable and I'd have to suffer the consequences … even if that meant losing him forever.

I started choking, gasping for air, anything to force air into my lungs. Carter had his hands on my face, his forehead pressed against mine. He was saying some gibberish I could barely hear as sweat was pouring down my skin. I couldn't see anything but blurs of Carter's face. My body was overheating, and I felt a wave of prickles erupting through my bloodstream.

"C-Carter … I …"

Squeezing my eyes shut, I tried to focus on the broken words through the congestion in my ears. None of it made sense. But when I tried to open my eyes again and tried to search for a new way of asking for help, there was no way out. I was falling down the tunnel and I couldn't fight back.

***

A cloth was on my forehead and I was laying flat on the couch. Carter was sitting on the edge, running his fingertips up and down my jawline. He paused when he saw my eyes open, there was a small smile on his lips. There wasn't anger … or even disappointment.

I had scared him.

Most importantly, I scared myself.

"You came to a while ago, but then fell asleep. It's almost noon."

I nodded. I had come downstairs at eight this morning.

He breathed in and I braced myself for the impact of his words.

"If I only have these last few hours with you, I don't want to waste them fighting. There will be plenty of time for us to be angry when we aren't under the same roof. But you say you still love me and I believe you. I still love you, too. So can we please, like we said we would, just pretend nothing is wrong? Celebrate the day like we wanted? And tomorrow we can pick up the pieces?"

His words started out strong but got weaker with each syllable. I was grateful for his words though. I didn't think I had it in me to fight anymore. But I did have it in me to love him like hell because I wasn't certain I'd ever have another chance.

My biggest mistake would be letting Carter James Morgan go.

So we did as we had planned. We microwaved our coffee and new cinnamon buns, and then the two of us sat in front of the Christmas tree, sorting through the gifts that actually were for each other. They were simple things, like clothing, socks, and underwear. We had reached that moment in our relationship and it only added more fuel to my fire. Carter recognized it too—apologizing with each gift that I opened.

I was certain neither of us would be using these gifts. We shouldn't have even exchanged them, just returned them instead.

There was a steady snowfall by the time we decided to make some lunch—a simple option of grilled cheese and tomato soup. We had a big dinner with Carter's closest friends that evening, so we didn't want to eat too much. We both sat at our kitchen table that overlooked our sanctuary. Our backyard was a lush, green wilderness that we loved exploring and now, despite the dead trees, we had a winter wonderland at our doorstep.

"Do you remember every snow day when we would alternate which house would get a snowman? We'd spend hours in the snow and without fail, each time we'd come in soaking wet, our parents would have this lunch prepared?" I offered the memory, my grilled cheese needing to be swallowed down with some soup.

"Honestly, with all the kids our parents always had around, it was the cheapest option for them." He laughed.

And it's true. Between seven children and snow days, our parents had their hands full. We always had plenty of snowmen hanging around as well.

"Carter?" I finished up my sandwich, brushing my fingers over the plate. He swallowed before looking over at me. "What are we doing on New Year's?"

He shook his head.

"We aren't discussing this right now." His voice was almost robotic.

"We have to—" I started and he held up his hands.

"No, please. Just …" he sighed.

His elbows came to the table and his face fell into his hands.

"I'm right on the edge. There's only so much I can do today. So please, don't ask me to do anything more."

My chest ached and I found myself massaging my neck for lack of something to do. There were important things we needed to discuss—frankly before I left. I hated the idea of leaving so many things unsaid. But today was about him, focusing on what he needed. My worries could wait.

"Wanna go run around outside? Make a snowman for old times sake?"

A few more hours of avoidance wouldn't hurt, right?

He nodded and instead of us changing into warmer clothes, we both just put our winter jackets, hats, gloves, and boots on. In seconds, our pajamas would be soaked through, but I knew, at least for myself, that this would take the pain away momentarily.

Stepping out on the deck, I reached for his gloved hand. We interlaced fingers and paused. For just this moment, the two of us could breathe the same air in, close our eyes, and transport ourselves back to happier times.

We had found our own safe haven. We were both so excited when we were able to purchase this home. And now I was walking away from it. Would he stay? Should he stay? Would I be back?

His hand jerked me forward, pulling me out of my thoughts as we trampled down the steps and into the snow.

There was already a few fresh inches, but not enough for a snowman—not yet. So instead, we decided to walk further into the forest. Maybe nature would be able to fix me, remind me that this is where I needed to be, who I needed to be with.

The snow was falling lighter as we walked between the trees, only a few snowflakes filtering between the branches. Our hands were gripped tight. The only noise we could hear was the crunching of our boots.

We found our place—silly to call it that considering it was behind our house—but it was a tree we loved to sit up against and look out at the small pond—frozen now—of course. Our first spring here it was filled with stunning wildlife and extraordinary bright flowers. We hadn't expected to come across any water in our trail, so we felt it was special just for us.

I glanced over at him right before we stopped. His cheeks were rosy and his lips recently moistened. He never learned to not bite his lips in the winter. We often got into petty arguments about him stealing all of my chapstick every winter—this year he had already stolen three. I led us over to the tree and gently positioned him up against it. Before he had a moment to protest, I pressed my dry lips against his, bringing my gloved hands to warm his cheeks.

He hesitated, and I pushed him further against the tree before he gave in. For two people who were acting like nothing was wrong—we were pretty shit at it.

I could so easily get lost in his lips— in the taste of him, in the way that his hands held me close, the way his head angled just slightly, the way he breathed through the kisses, and when he'd get too caught up in the passion that he'd forget to, and all of a sudden, he'd exhale all at once. I had memorized every single thing about his kisses. And there was comfort in that. But it wasn't because I was too comfortable—I could make that work, we could find fire again. It was that I didn't know if this was everything I needed.

I was being selfish, but I also wasn't. It was easy to turmoil into the spiral if I let myself believe that I truly was selfish—believe me, I had time and time again. But I wasn't selfish. Knowing and accepting my identity is different than knowing exactly what I have to then go look for someone to give me something more. No one could compete with Carter—except maybe the other gender. There was a fine line I was treading, partially why it took me so long to say anything about it. I didn't want to come off as greedy or undeserving. Most days I was certain—regardless of gender—that no one could come close to what Carter gave me. But it was that *what if* in the back of my mind that would grind its way through and consume my entire being if I let it. And I finally had.

Our hands were underneath our jackets by now, heavy shallow breaths escaping through our lips, creating a fog around us. Shivering with exposed skin and desperate passion, this was the most loving we had been with each other in weeks.

Prior to him catching me, I distanced myself so much that we hadn't slept together in about four weeks. Today would be the fifth. Were we going to change that? Could we? Without killing the other?

I briefly pulled away, locking eyes with Carter— searching and hoping we could be reckless for a few moments longer. His fingertips played with my waistband and before he could go further, I was yanking him away from the tree, running back toward the house.

We were laughing and running, our hands locked together, skipping our steps up the deck and sliding the screen door violently open until we were inside where the warmth of the wood stove burned our skin.

Stumbling, we both began to strip as we made our way to the stairs. Carter fell face first into a step as he tried to shake his last pant leg off.

"Fuck!" He laughed, pulling his pants off before I gripped his arms, standing him up. We were both just our boxers and socks.

I guided his head down and pressed a kiss to his forehead that was already spotting red.

"You okay?" He nodded, but he closed his eyes momentarily.

I was losing him and fast.

"Last one to the top is a bottom." It was my favorite game to play with him. I always let him believe that he beat me, but I always preferred bottom.

This time was no different. His face flashed over into his competitive side and in a countdown of three, two, one, we bolted up the stairs. He elbowed me, right at the top, enough to slow my stance, but not enough to have me catapult backward. In a quick motion, he made it to the top step and then reached behind to grab my hand.

It was his favorite move.

Carter picked me up, throwing me over his shoulder as I screamed for him to let me down. This had all started one day when I was being stubborn and angry at him for no reason—this entire skit: from the race to our bedroom. That it had become a tradition of ours. Honestly, the view over his shoulder was one of my favorites.

The moment we entered the room, the air was thick. I tried to laugh harder, tickle his backside, crack a joke or two, but when he threw me down on the bed, his eyes glazed over. This was the last time I'd enter *our* bedroom.

The way he climbed onto the bed, hovering over me, with pain etched into his retinas, and worry knotted in his brows, was a brand new experience. The desperation clouded his often seductive, playful features. Each touch, every kiss, each moan felt like it would be the last time we ever experienced it. Through our heavy breathing, we massaged and clawed, bit and kissed, cried and laughed. When we both finished—in sync like we often could—we collapsed into each other, letting our tears mix with the pool of sweat between us.

*** *

"We shouldn't be doing this, Carter. We can fool ourselves, but our friends?"

We made love again or tried to, as both of us fumbled through our tears, anger, frustration, and pleasure. Insults spewed through his lips and aggression formed in my touch. We gave up in an exhausted defeat, both of us at our weakest. If it weren't for our minds shutting off for us, we both would have done something we regretted.

After a solid two hours of sleep, we showered before our dinner. The day was getting away from us and I wasn't ready to see tomorrow's sun, despite the ice in the air.

With both of us dressed in our ugly Christmas sweaters, we started to bundle up, collecting our winter belongings throughout the house.

"We can tell them tomorrow. Or next week. Or later. I just don't want to ruin anyone's Christmas."

"Wouldn't they be more upset that we lied to them?" I zipped up my jacket, tightening my scarf around my neck. "Carter, you can't even look me in the eyes. How can we lie to anyone?"

"They'll understand, Aidan." His voice was strained as he spoke my name.

Ever since we woke up from the nap, we avoided each other. Taking multiple steps in different directions just in case we were to bump paths.

But I dropped the conversation, grabbed our bags of gifts, and we walked out of the house and into his car.

The drive was silent, the last thing we needed was to kill each other before we arrived. My mind was running a mile a minute as I racked my brain for any common ground that hadn't been tainted. What could we do to pull this off? But by the time that we drove up, we were the last guests to arrive and I still didn't have a plan.

I could hear him taking a deep breath, just as I was, before we both exhaled and exited the car. I took his hand in mine—suddenly forgetting how we normally acted in public. Did we usually hold hands? Were we affectionate in front of our friends? How often did we kiss in public? Did we ever even touch?

His rigid form was not lost on me, as if he was repelled by my very presence. I know I was.

Before I could speak to him, the front door opened, and I heard squealing coming from inside before anyone appeared in the doorway.

"Guys, Carter and Aidan are here!" Georgie, who opened the door, yelled.

Carter let out strew of 'fucks' under his breath, shoving my hand away. His pace quickened, and his left hand slapped his face before violently gripping his hair. I ran to catch up to him, trying to grab his hand discreetly, but the glare he shot my way challenged me to make one more move.

Carter James Morgan has only been violent once in his entire life and it was to protect me from a bully in high school. He was suspended for a week for hospitalizing the bully. Aside from that, Carter has never hurt a fly—and wouldn't. He literally helps them escape back outside.

But now? Now that violence was directed at me. One more move on my end and we'd both live to regret it. *That* would sever the twenty-three-year bond.

Our friends were all swarming the doorway by the time we made it there, each person holding a drink and oblivious to the tension between me and Carter.

"Come on in!" Georgie said.

The crowd parted but all eyes were still on us. Carter, on the other hand, had his eyes bugged out and was shaking his head 'discreetly.' I didn't know what was going on, but if someone didn't explain what was happening soon, I'd be the one to lose it.

The front door closed, but everyone remained in position. Often times, we could sneak in and make our rounds. No one ever greeted us by the door.

"So? Let us see! Was it romantic? How'd it happen? Did you expect it? Did you cry?"

Everyone's eyes were on me, so I took a chance and looked up at Carter, brows furrowed. He was pale with a layer of sweat on his hairline.

"Carter?" I whispered. I tried to take his hand again, knowing that he wouldn't try a thing in front of his friends, but he shook it away.

"Holy shit," Braydon exclaimed. "You said no."

I heard murmurs throughout our friends. They were all discussing whatever the hell was happening. But I could only focus on Carter who looked about ready to faint. As I tried to reach out again, he shrugged me off, walking toward the kitchen. I couldn't find it in me to follow.

Bottles clanked against one another before the sliding glass door in the back of the house opened and then slammed shut.

I was growing lightheaded at the commotion. I could hear my heartbeat in my ears. I tried to flex my hands as they grew clammy in my gloves—desperate for the material to absorb the moisture. Everyone hovered closer to me in the small foyer, but now in complete silence.

"Can someone please tell me what the fuck is going on?" I screamed, turning toward everyone.

Each and every person stood up straight, their faces full of sorrow and confusion.

The room was closing in on me and I started to back up, finding space between me and the crowd. I swallowed the bile threatening to escape.

"A.J.," Georgie said softly, her arm coming to my bicep. "Did you say no to Carter's proposal?"

Fuck.

fuck.

FUCK.

I ran into the wooden chest right next to the door and sat down on it. I unzipped my jacket and ripped off my gloves, angrily wiping my hands on my jeans. Anything to help me breathe.

"M-marriage proposal?" I choked.

I wasn't dumb, but maybe, just maybe it was a different proposal. Perhaps, a business proposal.

With just a soft nod, the air in my lungs escaped. My head collapsed into my hands as I curled into myself. My stomach was churning, begging me to give in.

"Did he not ask?" Everyone's silence, except for Georgie's, was excruciating. I could almost hear Carter pacing through the panels of the deck.

"No," I swallowed.

I saw her hand coming toward me out of the corner of my eye and before she could comfort me, I brushed it aside.

Standing up, I took Carter's route. Instead of grabbing a beer, like it sounded he did, I grabbed us two glasses, pouring them both with scotch. Our friends kept their distance, not a footstep to be heard as I prepared our poison. I hated scotch, but something was telling me that this would be the best burn I'd feel in a while.

Right before I made it to the sliding glass door, I vomited over the trash bin, raising the glasses above my head. Before I started again, as I knew was sure to happen, I stood up straight, and wiped the remnants from my mouth on my jacket.

The air felt colder when I opened the door, highlighting the nervous sweats that consumed my being, helping me feel less claustrophobic in the confines of my clothing.

I was right, he was pacing back and forth on the deck. His steps only halted when I closed the door behind me.

I offered a scotch in peace. He took it willingly, drinking all the liquid in one go.

"I guess you heard," he mumbled.

Before I had a chance to speak, he was opening his mouth again.

"While I was making plans for the future, you were making plans to leave." The distaste in his voice brought tears to my eyes. He seemed calmer now, the air helping him as well. But I couldn't stop my mind from imagining him throwing me off this deck. I definitely deserved it.

"We hadn't discussed it in so long."

"Should we have to?" He screamed, throwing the empty glass, just centimeters shy of my face.

I ducked and watched as the snow caught its fall, leaving it in one unsatisfied piece.

Okay, maybe he wasn't calmer.

"We've been together for twelve years, Aidan! Twelve! In just a few months it'll be thirteen. So, sorry if I didn't know I had to discuss our engagement with you. Up until a week ago, I had no doubt that you'd say yes. I thought your moods were just because things weren't progressing."

I took a sip of the scotch. As it burned the back of my throat, I made the decision to throw it back in one go. Tears escaped my eyelids as I tried to contain my coughing.

"I don't know what to say anymore," I whispered.

I was exhausted by this situation, by myself, by the person I had become and was trying to become … this was just the beginning.

"I feel like I have no say in this. I can't make any decisions."

"They aren't your decisions to make!" I yelled back, closing the distance between us.

Why couldn't he understand that? If he wasn't careful, *I* may push him off the deck.

"No." His words were soft. "No, they aren't. However, a little warning would have been nice. I'm not broken from a cheating lover. That I can heal with time. I'm heartbroken because I've lost complete trust in the closest person I've ever known."

I almost wish he did push me off the deck.

I rushed over to the railing, leaning over, and I emptied the remains in my stomach. I continued to retch, gripping the railing with my bare hands—forcing myself to feel the way my fingertips were growing numb.

Carter's hand came to my back. He rubbed up and down only once before he positioned me in front of him.

I could see his tears reflecting in the golden light from the house. He was challenging my eye contact. His gloved hand cupped my cheek and his thumb trailed over my lips. Carter leaned in, pressing a kiss to my forehead. The cool breeze that drifted over the moisture he left ignited my tears to fall.

"I want you out by the morning. You don't have to take all your belongings yet until you find a place. You can keep a key until you do. Call your family and reschedule a Christmas with them and I'll do the same. I … I hope you find what you're looking for. I hope you do go see a therapist. I … I hope maybe when the time comes, we can be friends again. But right now, right now I need you to go."

I wanted to argue and say that I had every right to stay, but truth is, I didn't. These were his friends, I only got to know them through him. My friends from work had another party a few days from now.

"Take my car home and make your plans. I'll get a ride back from someone here."

He reached into his jacket pocket, pulling out his keys. Before handing them to me, he took the house key off the ring. Carter then pulled me into a hug.

"I love you," I cried, burrowing my head into his neck.

"I love you too." He pressed a kiss on my hair and then let me go with a gentle shove.

Without another glance, he walked away. He picked up the glass he threw first before heading inside.

One glance indoors, I saw his frame surrounded by his friends. In the matter of minutes, they would learn about what I did. They'd form their opinions, they'd curse me out, they'd tell me he could do better and move on. Worst of all, I could second every single person's opinion of me.

I placed my glass in the snow on the deck ledge before descending the steps and walking around the house to Carter's car.

✳✳✳

When I pulled into the driveway, I had already made the decision to drive back to my hometown. It was the worst punishment I could place upon myself, yet it would be rewarded with the most support.

I had to pull the damn bandaid all the way off if I wanted to get Carter back in my life faster. So, I packed as many bags as I could, taking more than just my clothing, shoving it all into my small car.

I'd have to leave things—it was inevitable. He could throw it all to the curb if he pleased. There'd be no room for it at my parent's home anyway.

Right before I left, I packaged all my family's Christmas presents up. A small box with an envelope attached tumbled out from behind the tree.

It was wrapped to perfection, but I knew what it was. He had hidden it from me—but possibly even further under the tree this afternoon. Carter had been the one distributing the gifts, he had the control.

Every ounce of energy I had left in me was used as I forbid myself to rip the wrapping. I wanted to see what the future could look like. Maybe if I could feel the ring on my finger? Admire it? Imagine us at the alter?

I *had* imagined every last detail of our future. We had planned everything already—together. It was true, we hadn't spoken of our engagement in quite some time. But he was right, we had spoken about it extensively, why would he need to bring it up again, if he were planning a surprise?

But how would he have done it? Would it have been over breakfast? Were we supposed to go somewhere this afternoon? Maybe an engagement by the pond?

I shook my head, throwing the ring back under the tree as if it were a bomb. I couldn't do that to him. Not after everything else I'd done.

But the ring got caught on a tree branch, ripping the taped envelope off. It fell right in front of me.

My Love was written in Carter's cursive.

That was a sign, right? The envelope wouldn't be as painful as seeing the ring.

Tentatively, I opened the envelope and pulled out a crisp white note card.

Dear Aidan,

I want the security of knowing that I can give you everything I have. I need those deep brown eyes of yours to always look at me. Always look into me. Always hold my glance and encourage me.

I want to peel back piece by piece, every single layer until I reach the core of who you are. I want to know everything. Not just the present or the future, I want the past. I want to know what has led up to this day that you stand before me.

I need your gritty, depressing spirals and your exciting, extraordinary memories. I want to be able to channel you through just one look—my look. I need to be able to convince you that you're worthy of feeling loved in a way you've never felt before.

I want you to know with just a glance that I find you absolutely irresistible and that you, singlehandedly are capable of being able to change my life with your opinions, thoughts, and ideas.

But above all, I want and need to look into your eyes and see your light shine on, not because you're where I want you to be, but because you're where you want to be.

-Carter

Dropping the letter, I pressed my fists into my eyes and let out an agonizing scream. I screamed until my lungs ached and I fell forward, connecting my head to my thighs and muffling my cries.

How could I be so stupid? What was wrong with me? Why couldn't this be easier? Why *couldn't* he help me with this? I could fix it, I could fix it all right now. Just go back to the party and tell him I'm sorry, that I made a mistake, that it was him all along.

But it isn't him, at least, maybe not.

I gripped my hair, pulling at the strands, trying to stop my thoughts from spiraling. I rocked myself back and forth on my shins, trying to find some sense of peace.

In an instant, I shot up in realization. Today was a mistake. There was no way I could spend one more night here, staring up at the guest bedroom ceiling, wondering when it'd be morning. Instead, I needed to stare directly into the darkness, hoping my headlights were enough to guide me to safety.

So, I made a list. How do I get from point A to point B?

Grab gifts, return key, get in car, and drive. Taking the note, I placed it in my back pocket and stood up. I repeated those four things like a broken record until I found myself behind the wheel—my house key hanging from our key ring right inside the foyer. Flurries started up again as my thoughts began to tangle while I drove the long, icy highway on Christmas. Each mile driven, the note card seemed to weigh heavier in my pocket. Just a single reminder that I was driving away from the one place that would forever be my true home.

Hidden | *Sam Baker*

The bitter wind was sharp

like razor blades against my skin

—dense and unforgiving

 like the endless winter was.

But it wasn't the wind that frightened me.

It was the snow,

rolling, drifting, piling on the ground

—smothering, crushing, falling.

As I prayed for some escape

from this wretched place,

I stood among the falling, frozen flakes,

their sharp edges tearing my face.

Before it was too late,

before I drifted away,

I had to know.

What was hiding beneath

the unforgiving snow?

In the Snow | Sam Baker

The scream that echoed from outside my window jolted me awake. I thought at first it was a dream, something that came creeping from my unconscious to haunt me in my sleep, something that sounded so much like a call of terror that once escaped my throat one Christmas morning when I was a child. But as I sat in bed, barely awake, with the cold drool dripping down my cheek, it still pierced through the air.

And as it continued in a high pitch that sounded like my kid neighbor, Tommy Reed, I knew I was awake. The sad truth was that the screaming was such a regular part of our lives that anyone else would have gone back to sleep. But I was the Village Trapper, one of them anyway, and it was my job to keep the order, to wake and run at the alarm of a screaming child.

The scream abated as I rolled out of bed and searched for my boots on the dark wood floor of my cabin. But I didn't let the silence fool me as I wrapped a thick scarf around my neck. Whatever was causing the terror was likely still very much alive. I had done this too many times in the last few days to count. It was the week before Christmas when the screams and shrieks could be heard too often in the middle of night. So I shrugged on my heavy, wool-lined coat and grabbed hold of my rifle like clockwork as I headed for the door.

Our village, Winterville, was the smallest one in our cluster. We were poorer and less populated than the other villages around, so our few walking paths only consisted of packed dents from sled marks in the thick layers of snow. And it snowed so often that I had to make a new path every few days.

The lantern light glowing from Tommy's cabin was my beacon as I trudged through the thick snow toward him, trying not to get stuck within the heavy white powder in the process. A shadow of what looked like a running toddler danced across the side of the house. But as I looked again, allowing my eyes to adjust in the darkness, I saw nothing other than the thick ring of snow that circled the cabin. Two neighbor kids scurried from across the way as I stood in front of Tommy's cabin. They were no doubt eager to see what was going on.

But they weren't frightened like the younger children would be. These were teenagers who climbed up the porch of Mrs. Reed's house behind me, the house that her son Tommy slept in, as if they didn't want to miss the show, the one that had been a familiar occurrence in this village for too many years now.

I hated that those kids treated it like a game, that they couldn't curb their curiosity for little Tommy's sake, for his mom's sake, for all the other kids in the village's sake … for my fucking sake. Although they didn't look like it, they were still just kids, trying to make a game out something, anything, because it was the only way to stay sane in this frozen village that we all tried to call home.

"Go back to bed," I said to the kids as I knocked on Mrs. Reed's front door.

They snickered as they lingered by the door longer, but the shorter of the two stepped back quickly and pulled the other away as I shot them a threatening glare. I was the Trapper, and they knew I could make sure neither of them got their Christmas presents this year if I wanted.

I pulled my hand up to knock on the door again, but it opened before I had the chance to, and my fist fell through the air. Mrs. Reed was standing inside the house as she held the door open, and she pulled me in quickly by the arm as if she didn't want to be seen. It was probably good she wasn't seen because her face looked so horrific that it could have given one of the village kids nightmares for years to come.

I was worried about Tommy, having to look at his mom's face like that. I couldn't help but feel sorry for him as I stepped into the house and waited for Mrs. Reed to close the door. I stood in front of her as I looked for Tommy in the front room, as if to block him from being able to see his mom's fright. Often, it was the parents who overreacted about the things that went on the week before Christmas. But despite her broken, twisted, and tear stained face, Mrs. Reed was calm just like Tommy needed her to be.

Tommy was sitting in the rocking chair by the fireplace with his mom's quilt wrapped in thick bundles around his body. She made that quilt not long after he was born. I remembered watching Tommy for her while she stitched the squares together, making patchwork out of torn scraps. As the Village Trapper, I did more than just protect. I helped watch the babies, fixed broken gutters, patched holes in the roofs, ran to the cries of children at night, and took care of the thing that made them cry.

I was immediately looking around the open space of the living room as I walked toward Tommy, trying to figure out what made him scream like he did. He held his face over a cup of warm cider, the kind that the Grocer brought by each house at the beginning of the week to give the kids something to drink other than water. It was the only way they kept warm. Without it, their small bodies would freeze.

Mrs. Reed shuffled behind me as I came to Tommy, her thick skirt dragging on the scuffed floors, scraping chunks of ice behind her. Tommy looked up at me with wide eyes, eyes that I couldn't seem to get away from. They were locked on me now, and even as I shifted to crouch by his side, they followed. His eyes didn't frighten me though, it was the fact that I knew what he was feeling that sent shivers up my spine.

"Was it …" I paused as Tommy took a large gulp of the cider, his eyes watering as if it was too hot. "Was it the deer again?" I asked as I looked at him and gripped the strap of my rifle which hung on my back.

His hands shook as I said the words. Before I could stop it, the hot liquid poured over the rim of the cup, soaking into the bundles of quilt on his lap. And the tears fell onto his red cheeks as the chair swayed forward and back in his panic.

"Oh honey …" Mrs. Reed said as she quickly gathered the mug from him and pushed the wet part of the blanket off his legs.

"I'll get you something else … something not so hot," she said as she quickly wiped his tears on her sleeve as if the small water marks themselves were frightening.

Tommy shivered in the chair, and I knew it was because he was afraid. His small hands reached out to me as I turned and watched his mom leave the room to make her escape. She was too relaxed right now, in a way that seemed almost forced. It was like she was trying to pretend something that happened … didn't. And I stood up as I realized that there was no way it could have been the rabid deer bothering them this night … it was something else.

I wanted it to be the deer, I really did. Those deranged creatures caused only turmoil this time of the year. If they weren't tearing up the yam fields, they were terrorizing the villagers, ripping down their gutters, ramming into their back doors, or calling to them from the wintery darkness outside. But the house was calm, and only the soft wind brushing past the side of the cabin called from the outside. And I knew as Mrs. Reed made it to the kitchen and looked back at me, there was something else she needed to tell me, something she didn't want Tommy to hear.

"I'll be right back … okay Champ?" I asked as I tossed Tommy's hair out of his face and tugged the quilt back over his clammy hands. His eyes still followed, eyes that never seemed to blink, as if he was afraid of what he might see when he closed them.

I didn't need to hear Mrs. Reed's words to know what was going on, but I waited for her to speak anyway as I walked into the kitchen and stood with her by the wood stove.

"It wasn't the deer this time was it?" I asked as I leaned close to her, the heat from the stove warming my side.

"It wasn't," she said in a whisper as the tears trickled onto her face, something she corrected quickly by blotting them away with her sleeve.

I had known this woman for years, even before Tommy was born. After her husband, Han, died in the Great Snowfall, she did all she could to protect Tommy. She couldn't protect him from everything, but she could protect him from her tears, from knowing that she wasn't as strong as he thought she was.

"It's okay, Nancy," I said as I held onto her arm.

The Village Trappers protected, but they also cared. And this woman needed to be cared for as much as Tommy did. She was facing the stove as the tears crawled down her cheeks again, and they ran so quickly that one fell and sizzled onto the hot stovetop. She extinguished the stove quickly, glancing over at Tommy as if to see if he noticed she was crying.

I looked back too, but he was just sitting in the chair, buried in the quilt—rocking, like rocking was the only thing he knew how to do. As I saw the way he continued to act, the way Nancy's face was scattered and unsure, I was beginning to understand what was going on. But it was just a gut feeling then, and I didn't want to trust my gut.

"It wasn't the deer," she finally whispered as she grabbed onto my hand and pulled me behind the wall that separated the kitchen from the living room. Even in the short moment that we couldn't see Tommy, I was worried something was going to happen to him without supervision. I'm sure she was worried too.

"I don't know how it happened," she said as she brushed her palms nervously on her skirt. "We did everything like normal … I just don't understand … it's not fair …" she said as her voice became fragmented between sobs.

"What happened?" I asked in a low voice as I pulled myself closer to her to try and hear her words.

"I told him to wait. He always waited each year. But this year he didn't. I don't know. I keep forgetting that he's getting older and changing, that … he's not just a baby anymore. But this … this is going to change him forever," she said as she held her hands over her face as if she didn't want me to see her cry.

But her tears were merited. I knew that. I don't know if she knew that, but the tears continued to roll as I pulled her hands away, pleading her to remain calm with my stare.

"It's going to be okay. I know it doesn't seem like it right now, but it will. Just tell me what happened," I said as I let go of her hands and brushed off the tears on her cheek that she had become too distracted to blot away.

"After you checked our crate delivery yesterday, I put our gifts by the fireplace and told him that he had to wait until Christmas morning to open his. He knew he had to wait. But when I woke up to him screaming just now … he was standing over his gift. He had opened it and …" she paused as she gasped for air like she forgot how to breathe.

"And what?" I begged her to continue although I already knew I didn't want her to.

"And it was full of snow," she said as she bursted into loud sobs, so loud that I'm sure Tommy could have heard from the other room.

"Did he see, Nancy? Did he see what was in it?" I asked suddenly, hoping that if anything good would turn out from this conversation, she would at least say no.

But she nodded her head as she held her sleeves over her mouth, gnawing on them as if to stop herself from screaming.

"Where is it?" I tried to ask calmly, but my voice wavered.

I held onto her shoulder as if to comfort her, but really it was to hold myself in place as my knees shook. She pulled her arm in the air slowly as if it was weighed down by ice covered bricks and pointed to the back door. Wrapped in green paper by the door, in a puddle of water, was Tommy's present, the one that felt like it was full of feathers when I checked it the day before.

I felt like I was stumbling as I stepped forward, but I kept my knees as rigid as possible to allow myself to walk straight, to not fall, to not splash into the puddle of water that used to be snow, snow that was hiding something I didn't want to remember.

But I couldn't stop the memories this time. Like Tommy's piercing cry that woke me this night, another came to mind, one that sounded so familiar because it was my own, one that I couldn't help but allow to flood my ears again, causing me to lose track of the room around me, and pulling me into a time that was so far gone. But the scene was still crisp in my mind …

I was eight one Christmas morning when my parents woke me up early to open the gifts. It was dark then like it was most mornings before we were able to get the street lamps posted. And we were so poor that we didn't have wood to burn, so I sat on the fireplace with the lamp by my side to keep warm. I watched my shadow flicker across the wall of the cabin as my parents prepped breakfast together in the kitchen. Even though those were miserable times, and the food was scarce, and we knew the presents were going to consist of necessities instead of luxuries, my parents were still able to find happiness that morning.

But a great disappointment washed over me when I sat on the fireplace and realized how small my present was. There were three. The green box said, *"Caroline"* on it for my mom. The yellow one said, *"James"* for my dad. And the small blue one that hid in the shadow of the other two said, *"Nick"*. That was my present, and I pouted silently as I wondered why the Charity had given me a smaller gift than last year, probably smaller than the rest of the kids in the village.

Each person in the family received one gift every Christmas from the Charity, bought with the village's joint holiday fund. The other villages did it too, but I knew that they were able to afford more than one gift, something different than socks and blankets, and something more entertaining than balls of string that only the stray dogs found amusement from.

That's why I felt like I had a secret of my own when I saw the round, black box sitting in the fireplace. I didn't know how it got there … the fireplace had been completely empty the night before. But I didn't want to say anything because an extra box meant an extra present. And as a kid, I convinced myself that it was the other part of my measly gift that the Charity must have forgotten.

Because I didn't want my secret to be ruined, I crawled into the fireplace quietly while my parents weren't looking. I didn't even bother to look for a name tag because just for once, I wanted to be a rebellious kid who found some sort of excitement from opening things that might not belong to them. And even though I thought the gift probably could belong to me, there was a thrill I got from lifting that lid and feeling the familiar winter chill seep out from the box.

The snow was rough against my hands as they plunged deep into the box. I thought it was a game, like digging for treasure. In Winterville, the snow was our dirt. So, I just dug and dug and clawed my fingers into the snow until I felt something claw back. It was soft and mushy on one end, sharp and pointy on the other.

I thought it could have been a snail because of the hard shell like feel of the tip as I gripped onto it. And I couldn't help but wonder what kind of joke this was. Why was the Charity sending me a snail? Did they really think I was only worth a snail?

I pulled the … whatever it was out of the snow angrily because I hated snails, and I hated how gross and squishy they were, and this one already felt squishy and limp and wet. And when I yanked it out of the box and held it in the air, I realized … it was not a snail.

You might remember me telling you about the scream, but not the way it sounded, not the way it came out of my throat without filter or force, the way it made my tears rush even quicker down my cheeks. The chunky bits of bloody snow covered my hand as I held the severed finger in the air. I dropped it onto the dusty ground of the cabin as I realized how much it looked like my own finger, how much it felt so real like the ones still attached to my hands. I wanted to pretend it was fake, that it was some sort of prank pulled by village kids with too much time to waste. But the blood soaked into the floor, into the snow, into my pants as I tried to rub it off my chilly hand.

There was nothing my parents could do to stop the screams, so they just waited. And there was nothing the Charity could do to answer the problem other than to say that they only sent three boxes instead of four. And instead of the comfort that I needed so much as a kid, the reassurance that something as horrific as that would never happen again, I was only given unsure answers and looks of grief from my parents. But there was something other than the severed finger that still haunted me. It was a question that remained unanswered. If the Charity didn't deliver the fourth box … who did?

"Nick? Are you okay?" Nancy asked as she shook my shoulder.

I nearly forgot where I was standing, and I almost fell over as she grabbed my arm. But the warm touch of her skin brought me back to the present, a time that was almost as horrific as that night when I was a kid.

"I don't know how it's possible," Nancy whispered to me as if the words themselves could haunt.

"What?" I asked as I looked at the puddle of water gathering by my feet.

"I checked his box last night … there was the wooden train in it but not … not that," she cried as she stood behind me.

Her whispers haunted me even if she didn't intend them to. She was telling me that this gift, the one that sat in front of me now in a soggy mess, was different than the identical one that I brought into her house and checked the day before. If this wasn't the same gift, how did it get in there, and where was the one that it replaced?

"Nancy, I want you to listen to me," I said in a hurried voice as I stepped over the puddle of water. "You stay inside with Tommy," I continued as I reached down and pushed the lid of the gift box closed. I didn't need to see what was in it to understand that I didn't want to see it. I had removed twelve snow gifts this week. Enough was enough. "Don't let him out of your sight," I continued. This wasn't just any snow gift. Whoever or whatever left it was smart enough to figure out our system. They knew to wait until I wasn't looking, to switch the first box out with the new gift—one filled with snow and … other things. And somehow it got into her house unnoticed. "Keep the doors locked and don't let anyone other than me in. Okay?" I asked as I grabbed the box and shoved it under my arm.

"Why does this keep happening to our village?" she asked as she dried her face with her skirt.

She was another victim of the snow gifts. She found hers not long after mine. She knew what a cruel thing this was, a gift that still had so much horror to give after all these years. Her blonde hair that was pinned up in a high braid was falling in pieces against her shoulder.

"I don't know. But I'm going to stop it," I said as I turned to the back door and opened it.

"Be careful," she said as she grabbed my hand and then quickly let it go again.

"Remember, lock the door," I said with a nod as I stepped back into the snow and closed the door behind me.

We had a place where we dumped all the snow gifts. I was heading there when I realized it was still too dark to make the walk without my lantern. So before leaving to the pit, I turned and headed back toward my cabin to grab my light. The snow was easier to walk in now when the temperature had dropped a little and the top layer was turning into slush. The bottom layer though, remained as a constant shield for the dirt, the earth of our village that I had never really seen before. And I felt like it was built off layers and layers of old snow, scattered with ruins of the igloos that our great grandparents used to live in.

I was eager to rid myself of the gift under my arm that rattled as I shifted footing, but I realized I wasn't going anywhere else that night when I reached my front door and heard the low grumbled calls behind me. I froze for only a second as I wondered if they were real. But I knew that a second was all I had. I dropped the gift box as I lunged for the door and ripped it open.

When I found myself on the inside, I locked the door and slammed by body against it as the deer who tried to ambush me rammed into it, shaking the hinges. The sound of their antlers and hooves scraping against the outside of my house made my chest feel hollow. I didn't want to deal with this frightening thing, tonight of all nights. When the deer quieted, I opened the lookout window near the top of the door, so I could peer outside.

There were five of them huddling around my front porch. I inhaled slowly as my chest shook against the door. I could see their glowing green eyes, and I could hear their deranged growls as they approached the gift box on the ground like a pack of wild dogs. And that's exactly what they acted like. The hunted had become the hunter.

I heard stories when I was boy about how the deer used to be skittish and delicate creatures. These ones clearly didn't share those traits with their ancestors. I thought about shooting them to still my fears that night, but bullets were in short supply. We needed to save them for the more dangerous things, things that lurked around the village, sneaking into people's houses, and leaving severed body parts on their fireplace. I knew anyone who would do that posed a bigger threat than a pack of rabid deer.

But that's not to say the deer weren't dangerous. Out alone in the darkness among a pack of deer, no one stood a chance of survival. They had a vicious sort of way about them. Their kicks and rams were so powerful that they could knock a man's brains right out of his skull … I saw it happen years ago. And if they were given no other choice, they took to grabbing a hold of flailing limps and gnawing a person apart bit by bit. A quick shiver went through my body again. I would shoot them if I needed to, but I hoped the door would protect me, so the bullets wouldn't have to.

All I could do was watch in slight worry as they crowded and pushed each other around, each trying to get a good whiff of the crushed gift box on my porch. And eventually, a deer in the front knocked it over with its scarred and bloody nose, letting the contents spill out onto the snow.

Before I could stop myself from looking, I saw all of what Tommy did when he opened the gift that night. It was difficult to see at first under the darkened sky. But the red mixed into the white like snow cones gave it all away. Things came out of the box that I'd never seen before, parts that I was sure only belonged on the inside of a body, deep within the recesses of an abdomen.

But it all kept pouring like an unstoppable shower of gifts. And they just kept giving, kept seeping, and tumbling, kept … bleeding. There was an ear, a few fingers, and maybe an eye sitting on a sloshy bed of what could only be organs. Our secret gift giver was being generous this year. I tried not to gag as I kept looking out the door. And I was sure to remain quiet, so the rabid animals wouldn't catch me watching them.

I don't know how long it really was, but it seemed like thirty minutes that the deer got their full of the scraps from the gift box, wetting the fur around their mouths with blood. Like assorted candies, they sampled. Two of them fought over the ear by my array of miniature snowmen in the lawn, knocking them over as they scrambled to get the best and fleshiest parts of their snack. After lingering for a few more minutes, they walked in a pack away from my house. Who knew creatures who were once so solitary would find company when all instincts had been abandoned?

I held on nervously to the strap of my rifle as I waited to see which direction they would go. They were heading to a path that would lead them to Nancy's house. I would shoot them all in the dark before I let them terrorize her and Tommy that night. But they took a quick right as they continued, heading in a direction that was only miles of forest and tundra thereafter.

And although I wish that left me satisfied to know that one nuisance of the night was taken care of, it didn't leave my mind at ease. I shuffled through my dim cabin, feeling the counters and tabletops for my lantern.

And as I fumbled over the empty glass bottles and tin cans that were strewn across the place, I accidentally knocked my lamp over. I cursed as the glass shattered on the floor. I was thankful then to be wearing shoes. I knew that I needed to go find the other Trappers and tell them what happened, but the dimming light posts outside would only get me so far. I couldn't imagine going out in the dark and getting stuck in the snow on a night like this.

I sighed as I realized I would have to wait for first light, for another few hours that seemed like years to go. But I also knew that I needed rest, some sort of escape from this night, from the things I didn't want to remember about nights like these. I fell into the bed that felt too large for my body then, keeping my shoes and thick jacket on incase I needed to make a quick run again. And I held my rifle at my side in the chance that the deer would decide to come back.

Although I wish I was diligent enough to stay awake those few hours and listen for any more disturbances at night, to know that the village was safe and cared for, I let the sleep take me. It was sleep that was needed but not welcome. And while I slept, I saw things from Christmases past that I didn't want to see. The holiday that was looming so close only brought awful memories for me now.

I dreamt in fragments of those images—piles and piles of gift boxes all soaking out the bottom, green eyes creeping and looming behind me no matter where I went, skittering figures in the dark that were so quiet it could have almost just been the wind. I woke in a jolt like I did the first time that night, except for it was barely just morning as I saw the warm sunrise peek through the crack in my otherwise insulated door.

And like the first time waking that night, I heard a scream. But this time, it wasn't just one scream, it was about half a dozen, all coming from different parts of the village, each sounding more panicked than the first. As I was jumping out of the bed and strapping on my rifle, I heard the village bells ring. A meeting had been called. I ran out the front door as I saw Nancy carrying Tommy out in her arms, trying to keep her skirts off the snow as she shuffled along.

"Where are you going?" I asked as I shuffled to her quickly, being careful not to trip on the jutting chunks of solid ice in the path from our daily footprints in the snow.

"The meeting. I didn't want to be left alone over here while everyone else went to the center. Do you mind carrying him?" she asked with a sigh as she hefted Tommy in her arms carefully as if she was trying not to wake him.

"Sure," I said as I positioned him in my arms with his head resting on my shoulders like I used to when he was a baby.

It would have been better for them to stay inside, away from the cold and the possible threat of another deer sighting. But I also knew that she had things to say to the village. The story of what happened to Tommy last night would likely be matched with others. If the Barons heard about how serious our problem was, I was hopeful they would send more Trappers to help.

Tommy woke by the time we got to the village center. And although the tired bags under his eyes seemed heavy, he stomped playfully in the snow by Nancy's feet as we waited for the rest of the villagers to arrive. One by one, the families all gathered in from scattered directions. On this morning of Christmas Eve, there was not one happy face in the crowd.

The only calm face I found then was the Village Prayer. I don't know where she came from, and I'm not sure if anyone remembers, but she sat on the edge of the frozen fountain in her thick grey skirts like she did during every town meeting, and she held her head down as if in a prayer. I had never heard her speak, but her body said everything it needed to that morning. She held her head even lower then, as if she had heavier things to pray about. As we waited for the last Baron to arrive, I wondered how long it would take her to come to terms with the things she would hear this morning.

The Barons eventually filed in from the secluded places they called home. They were the lords who governed our village and made sure it was livable for the people. Their faces, mostly ones of seasoned men, were covered with worried wrinkles. I wondered if they knew how many lives had been changed this morning or if they heard all the screams of the children who would never know if they could trust Christmas again.

"It has come to our attention that there were snow gifts received this morning," the oldest of the Barons said as he looked up at the dim sky.

The villagers surrounding us nodded, and I immediately looked for the other Trappers in the crowd. They were there with their families, and the looks on their faces said that they knew they were done enjoying the holiday this year. Like most years, Christmas was our busiest time.

"If the time limit had been waited, it would have given the Trappers time to check the boxes before Christmas Morning. I warn you again, never open a box before Christmas Morning," the narcissistic raisin of a man said as he looked to the crowd like they were simply bothering him to just be a bother.

"Sir Baron," I interjected because I couldn't stand to listen to his nagging any further.

He nodded toward me to continue.

"The other Trappers and I finished checking all the boxes in the village yesterday. There were no extras, and there was no snow," I assured them as I stepped forward, leaving Nancy and Tommy to stand with the teenage kids I'd seen lingering by their house that night.

"Well how did so many of those awful gifts end up in the houses?" One of the other Barons asked as he adjusted his night cap and pulled his layers of heavy coats tightly around his body.

"That's what we've all been wondering," another Trapper, Robby, said. "I double checked Susan's present last night, but when I moved it this morning, it was packed full of snow."

"The same happened with Tommy's gift," Nancy confirmed.

"We'll just have to be more thorough with the gift inspections then," the third Baron said as he held a lantern in his shaky hand.

"*We* checked each family's boxes three times this year. There is no way we could have missed anything," the third

Village Trapper, Gerry, said boldly as he held firmly onto his wife's hand.

"Well then how did the bloody boxes get into the houses in the first place?" the first Baron, Terald, asked in a frustrated tone.

"That's the problem … we don't know," I finally said carefully as if to plead for the older men to listen.

"It must be some sort of bad magic. Maybe the Charity did this. They never favored us or our village!" one of the outraged Grocers said as he held a bag of rations at his side.

"Watch your tongue. The Charity is full of kind people who spend their time each year to orchestrate this holiday for you—ordinary people just like you," the second Baron, Eisle, said.

"In fact, many of our villagers work there. Are you meaning to say that our neighbors are trying to sabotage us?" the third Baron, Yonne, asked in an accusing manner as he turned down the glow of his lamp.

"No … I'm just saying, if that's where the gifts are coming from …" the Grocer replied reluctantly.

"Then what?" Terald asked in a sudden frustration. "Then they gave you generous gifts only to replace them with these insults later?" he asked.

The village center remained silent for a while after the Baron's words. I hated that he called the snow gifts 'insults'. It was like he never received one, never understood that they were so much more than that. They were a catastrophe, the thing ruining the only holiday we could afford to celebrate, something I'm sure the Baron's never had to worry themselves with anyway.

"If it's not the Charity, then who? Who snuck into my house last night and switched Tommy's present with a snow gift?" Nancy demanded as she walked with Tommy to my side.

"The Trapper who checked your gifts must have made a mistake. It happens to the best of us," Yonne said with a shrug.

I bit my tongue because I knew I couldn't take back what I was about to say. It was something so foul that I could be banished for the words. I clenched my jaw as I looked at Nancy. She slipped her hand into my grasp and squeezed. I didn't have to tell her what I was thinking. Somehow, I knew she understood that I wouldn't be negligent with something like that, especially for Tommy … especially for her.

"Even if that was the case," one of the village's Hunters began as she stepped forward. "Where are the snow gifts coming from?"

"Oh, sweet dear, you trouble us with a question we've never been able to answer. Quite an unfortunate thing isn't it?" Eisle asked in his normal belittling tone.

"So that's it. You're not going to do anything?" one of the teenage boys asked as he stood next to Tommy.

"There's nothing we can do, son," Terald said with a sigh as if he was grieved by the loss of innocence this night had seen.

"If you won't do anything, and we have no way of knowing when this will happen again, then we aren't opening any gifts this year," a paranoid father said as he held his daughter at his side.

"If that's what we must do to rid ourselves of this curse, then we won't either," another man said.

With some reluctance, the rest of the villagers agreed. The Trappers were to gather the rest of the presents that hadn't been opened yet. The people didn't want to be surprised again by the suddenly appearing nightmares that posed themselves as gifts.

"If that's what you must do to clear your conscious, then so be it. But don't be surprised if the Charity doesn't bring presents by next year after seeing what you're doing to the ones they just brought you," Eisle finally said as he turned from the villagers and walked back toward his home with Terald and Yonne following.

It was clear then that the Barons were never going to help. They were bitter old men who didn't know what the people needed in order to feel safe. I didn't believe that the gifts were turning bad because of some sort of dark magic. But the others tried to believe it because it was better than thinking that someone was somehow breaking into their homes, the only place they really felt safe, the place where their family slept. I didn't know what was more disturbing; the fact that I wanted to believe it was dark magic too, or the fact that I knew I couldn't.

"I'm sorry Nancy," I said as I turned to her. "I'll talk to the other Trappers and see if I can scrounge up some sort of gift for Tommy this year," I said quietly so the boy couldn't hear.

"No, it's okay … I'll just give him mine," she said as she turned and caught his hand in hers.

"Are you sure? Do you want me do check it again?" I asked as I wrapped my freezing hands within my scarf.

"It's fine. Thanks Nick," she said as she pulled Tommy into her arms again, his body wriggling in her grasp, and walked back toward her cabin.

It was the worst thing that could have happened. The children stopped smiling. They stopped laughing with mischief as they eyed their presents. Instead, they looked at them in grief like it was too hard to think about what might be inside, too difficult to pretend that they weren't afraid. Even the teenagers cried.

The other Trappers and I filled the village sled with the gifts from each villager's home. The ones we knew were packed tight with snow sat on the bottom, so that if the sled shifted, those would be the last to fall over.

"It doesn't feel right," Gerry said as he pushed the sled beside me. "Most of these are full of useful things, things we might need through the year. I know the villagers are worried, but we can't just throw them away."

"You're right ..." Robby said as he slowed on the path and looked to his house which wasn't far off. "We could put them in my shed and store them just in case."

Robby and Gerry were right. We couldn't throw away perfectly useful things, things that were bought with money that the village had provided together, things that could save us later in the year. We nodded in agreement, and Robby pulled the front of the sled up the hill to his house while Gerry and I pushed.

The door of his shed creaked open, cracking layers of ice that seemed to have remained undisturbed for at least a week. I helped them open the gifts quickly with the knife that I carried on my side. I slit each box open in a hurry, the wrapping tearing, ribbons bunching and then snapping against the sharp blade. We sorted the contents into the wood crates Robby had stacked against the walls—blankets, socks, hats, and cans of food. It was the same as last year, and like last year, it would keep us alive.

"I'll take the rest to the pit," I said as I pulled the handle on the sled, making sure the rest of the gifts, the ones full of slush and snow, didn't fall off.

"Are you sure?" Robby asked as he finished sorting the last few things from the gift boxes.

I nodded as I kept the shed door propped open with my foot, the ice cased on the bottom slipping past the side of my boot.

"Double check the rest of the houses and make sure that no more gifts show up. Any new ones after these are bound to be full of snow," I said.

I didn't have to mention what else they might be full of because the other two Trappers knew. I dragged the sled through the village out to the field that no one dared go, a place that was often scattered with preying deer, looking for scraps that I might leave behind. The pit was a deep hole in the ground, coated with snow on the inside so the frost and chunks of ice looked like teeth in the mouth of the earth.

And like a mouth, I fed it, dumping each gift down into the depths of the pit, looking away when they fell so I wouldn't have to see what fell out of them. But I could feel the rough snow, bits of rubbery … something sliding past my fingers—a grip of death.

Each year I had done the same, box by box, dumping them all in the pit, turning my head so I wouldn't see, but still accidentally catching a glimpse of something down in the snow when I looked back. And after all these years, it wasn't exactly what was inside the box that bothered me the most anymore. It was the two questions that lingered in my thoughts, the ones that still couldn't be answered. Where did the body parts come from? And who was sending them?

It was still dim out in the chilly morning sky when I turned away from the pit and yanked the empty sled back toward the village. I would try to forget about it all like I did every year. I would make sure the village stayed safe, keep watch for deer until they left during the spring. And I would keep telling myself that maybe, maybe if she could look past all this terror, that I could try to make Nancy happy again.

But I stopped walking as I neared the edge of the village when I saw something I knew was familiar. It looked exactly like the shadow I saw the night before, dancing across the outside of Nancy's house, the shadow that I mistook as an illusion. But when I saw it again, under the brightness of the morning sky, I knew it wasn't a shadow.

It was a figure, still small and dark, but it was moving quickly … running. And it was fleeing the village with something under its arm, something that I didn't recognize until it got closer. I didn't hesitate as I realized it was a present under the arm of the small thing. I immediately pulled my rifle into the air, wondering if the figure saw me. But I didn't shoot as I realized that this thing running through the snow away from the village looked as small as Tommy, could even have been Tommy.

But why run away from the village with a present? I breathed in a quick jolt as I realized it hadn't seen me yet. And I also realized there was only one reason to bring a present out of the village in such a hurry; it had just been replaced with another much heavier and colder one. I hid behind a pile of snow as I waited for the figure, whatever it was, to come closer to me.

As I heard the small plops of light footsteps, almost like a toddler shifting through the snow, I jumped out from behind the pile of snow and knocked the little thing off its feet in fright. I couldn't quite understand what or who I was looking at right away. I thought it could have been a village kid, but it was much too small, its skin much too green, and its left ear … much too missing.

The boy-like creature's face wrinkled in a pout as it turned on its stomach and tried to scramble away with the gift box in tow. But I grabbed him by the arm, noticing that two fingers on his left hand were missing in a bloody mess, sopped up with a thin green scarf. At first, the sight of the foreign, nightmarish thing that stood in front of me, it's whole body shivering, was haunting. But I quickly understood what I was looking at as I snatched the gift box out of his mangled hands and saw that there was a stuffed bear inside.

"Why? Why did you do this?" I asked suddenly as I dropped the gift box and yanked his arm in the air.

"Please … you're hurting me," he begged in a voice that sounded much too similar to a child's for my comfort.

But I knew with purple veins like his, wrinkly hands and arms, and the long, pointed nose that jutted out of his face, that he wasn't an innocent child. I didn't know what exactly he was … just not a child.

"Then answer me! Why are you doing this? Why are you stealing the gifts … and cutting off your fingers to leave for the kids?" I asked in a ragged tone because the words sounded so odd coming out of my mouth.

"You think … you think I wanted to do that?" he screeched as he curled the remnants of his fingers on his free hand and touched the spot on the side of his face where his ear used to be. "He … he makes us do it. I don't want to … but I have to," he said as he bursted into tears, tears that somehow reminded me of Tommy's from the night before.

I knew that it made no sense for this person … if that's really what he was, to cut of his own body parts to leave for the village kids. But he was still the one carrying the present and still the one running from the village in a suspicious hurry.

"Who makes you do this?" I asked as I loosened my grip on his arm and stooped down to his level.

I had so many questions that needed to be answered. Where did he come from? Who was he? *What* was he? And why had I never seen anyone like him before? But the most important question in that moment that needed to be answered was this: who sent him?

"Stanly," he said in a sigh as his body relaxed, nearly falling back into the snow.

"Who is Stanly?" I asked as I let go of his arm, hoping that he would know I didn't want to hurt him, that I was ready to listen to him, do anything I could to fix this problem that we both seemed to be suffering from.

"I can't just tell you who he is …" he said as the tears trickled onto the dark bags under his eyes.

"Why not?" I asked suddenly, flinching as I felt the small specks of snow hit the back of my neck.

"Because if he finds out …" he began.

"Then what? He'll cut off more of your fingers and force you to give them out like raffle prizes?" I asked.

"Or worse … he'll leave me for the reindeer," he said with a squeal.

"The reindeer?" I asked.

"Oh … but it's too late anyway. He'll leave me out and forget me now," the creature said as he shivered, nearly falling over from his shaking knees.

"He made you do all of this? This Stanly person?" I asked calmly, although my whole body felt tense.

He nodded as his twig like arms latched around his body. I think he realized he had no chance to run and escape me. And he was too late to go back to wherever he came from without consequences.

"I'm not going to hurt you," I promised as I took my scarf off and wrapped it around his bony shoulders. "And if you can show me where Stanly is, then I can stop him and make sure that you never have to deal with him again. How does that sound?" I asked.

He nodded sheepishly as he looked down at his feet, feet that I realized just then were only wrapped in bits of flannel. I should have gone back for the other Trappers, but I had worries that they couldn't answer. They might think to kill this creature. Or they might not have believed that this

Stanly person was real, still holding onto the idea that dark magic was a much better reason for all of this.

And if I waited much longer, I knew that Stanly, whoever he was, would realize one of his servants had yet to return. He would be even more suspicious as the time passed. And I also did this alone in the case that if this was all a lie, I could save myself from the embarrassment of anyone knowing that I trusted some crazed looking … thing about a questionable story like this.

The creature had a name. He called himself Red. And he said he was an 'elf'. His brothers and sisters were elves, too. Everyone he knew other than Stanly was an elf. I didn't really know what an elf was, but I gathered from the looks of him that it was some mutated, inbred form of a human. I didn't want to believe his story at first, but I also didn't know what to believe. After all, he was giving me some sort of explanation that was more concrete than 'dark magic'.

He was taking me to Stanly, so I continued to listen to him as he led the way, me pushing and him sitting in the sled as the words kept twirling out of his mouth like a bitter wind. They couldn't be stopped. I listened carefully to what he said, trying to determine how much of it was really true.

Red didn't know where Stanly came from. He just knew that he was always there. I still wasn't sure where exactly 'there' was, but Red said that Stanly lived in a large tower to the north. So, we went north.

"That's where he'll be," Red said in his squeaky little voice, almost as if he was afraid to say the words out loud, as if Stanly could somehow hear his betrayal.

Stanly was just one man with far too many gifts to give. He was generous, and he wanted to give even more than his own skill allowed him. Red said that Stanly was the first to pass out a sacrifice; the front two fingers on Stanly's left hand had been missing since before Red could remember.

From what I gathered, Stanly was a man with strange hobbies … obviously. But he didn't speak much, and according to Red, he was almost completely deaf in both ears. He was a hermit who never went outside. And he was clearly bitter.

Because he had so much to do, with so little time, the elves helped him pass out his gifts, sharing his craftsmanship to all the villages around. And not only did the elves hand-deliver the packages to the villagers' houses, they supplied the materials for each custom made … or rather custom grown gift.

Red was one of the oldest elves, although I still wasn't sure exactly how old that was. He had sacrificed a few of his toes for his younger siblings, taken lashes and beatings before for their mistakes. He just wanted to protect them all against the man who was *supposed* to protect them.

That's why he was running away from the village in the early morning. One of his smaller and weaker sisters, Sera, fell and hurt herself before delivering her package the night before. He had to deliver her gift too, so she wouldn't lose her nose. He was a good brother, the best one could ask for in a situation like that.

Stanly would take his dues quickly and move on to the next. It was all about business he'd say. But Red and the other elves never really knew what the business was all about. They had no idea why Stanly insisted on sharing parts of them with the rest of the world.

They would often stand in a line in the top room of the tower, and Stanley would come by with a sharp blade, swinging it to see how many of their fingers he could cut off in one swipe.

I looked at Red's bloody hand as he told me the details of his loss, wondering if it all could be real, or *how* it was real. Each elf had to pay a price at the end of the year right before Christmas. But this year, the price changed. The year before it was only one body part, but with supply and demand … the price doubled. Stanly didn't kill them if they paid their dues. But the ones who refused or ran out of parts to sacrifice … well, they were sent to the richer villages in even larger boxes.

I stopped the sled suddenly as Red told me this part. I sat next to him on the sled, stolen from breath, and a part of me didn't want to believe it was true. I couldn't believe it because it was so awful that something like that could be true.

But I knew it. I knew it as I looked at Red's bruised skin, his blood caked arms, and the eyes that were nearly bulging out of his sockets as if Stanly had already tugged on them to see how loose they were. I knew it from the shiver that escaped his body, begging for warmth that the world couldn't give him. I knew it was true.

As we sat there for a moment next to each other and I looked over to him wrapped in my scarf, he reminded me of Tommy. He was small and innocent and begging for love of any sort, begging for someone to show him that he was alive, as if he wasn't sure if it were really true. He was lost, falling apart, drying up in this cold world that had somehow decided he was the prey. This became more than just me and my village. If Red was telling the truth, I knew I couldn't let this happen anymore.

"How much further is it?" I asked as I stood up and started pushing the sled with Red still on it.

"Almost there," he said.

It had been hours since we started heading north on the tundra. As we skirted the forest to our right, I couldn't help but feel like I heard a faint call in the air. I tried to tell myself it was just the wind, but I worried it was something else.

This was the furthest out of the village I had ever gone. I was worried about so many things as I pushed on. I worried that I didn't bring enough bullets, that the deer would find us and overpower me the longer we were out on the open tundra. I worried about confronting Stanly, the person who, according to Red, did all the severing and slicing of body parts on his own, praising it as an art. I worried that I would get lost, or worse that Red was leading me to my death. And I was worried that I would never get to see Nancy again, never get to tell her how I really felt about her or ask if she felt the same.

"There it is," Red said as he stood up from the sled.

The tower stood a few hundred yards in front of us, massive in size, stripped and spotted with black tar coating the sides of the brick structure. The front of the building was crumbling and unkempt with slopes of snow gathering under the eaves.

"That's where Stanly's at?" I asked as I stopped in my tracks.

But I was distracted by something else, something I didn't quite notice until we got closer and closer to the tower. There were ice covered pods sticking out from the ground. In fact, they weren't just covered in ice, they were made of it. And inside were smaller creatures that looked just like Red, curled in the fetal position as they slept.

"What is that?" I asked as I sucked in a jagged breath.

"They're not ready yet. They aren't strong enough to leave," Red said as he pressed his hand on the outside of the closets pod and peered in.

"Are they …" I began.

"They're elves too, like me. This is how we're born," he explained as he stood back up and shrugged the scarf back over his shoulders.

"Who are your parents?" I asked, because I had no idea how something like this was possible.

"Stanly is our only parent," Red said as he looked toward the tower.

I knew he was scared. He was turning against a man who had used power to hurt him. And he probably thought that power would back lash and find him again one day. But I was going to make sure that didn't happen. I didn't know how it was possible for the elves to live like this, to be born like they were. But as I looked at Red, as I remembered that finger I saw in my gift as a kid, as I remembered how real it felt, I knew he didn't deserve this at all … none of them did.

"Do you have the key to get in?" I asked as we stayed still by the sled.

"You don't need one," Red assured me.

"What do you mean?" I asked.

"It's unlocked," he said as he leaned against the sled.

"How does he keep you from running away?" I asked.

"He doesn't have to. We have nowhere else to go … no place to keep warm … no one to feed us," he said.

I was torn by his words. How awful was the world we lived in, that going out into the cold winter alone was worse than torture and losing body parts?

"Will you show me where he is?" I asked.

Red shook his head quickly. "I won't go back in there. He'll kill me if he knows what I've done. But you can find him. He's just at the top of the tower. Follow the screams," Red said as he covered his blue lips with my scarf.

Follow the screams.

It was the exact opposite of what I wanted to do. But instead of the screams calling to me, it was the low and grumbled snarls that I unfortunately knew so well. To the right, on the edge of the forest, a pack of the snarling, panting, deranged deer lurked.

"We have to go!" I said as I picked Red up in my arms.

I knew he wouldn't be fast enough to outrun the deer, so I held him as we ditched the sled and ran straight toward the tower. But Red wriggled in my arms like Tommy would. Now was not the time to protest.

"Stop! Stop!" Red yelled in my ear, so loud and screeching that I felt deaf for a moment.

"What?" I asked as I tried to keep hold of him.

But he was out of my grasp and running back toward the deer in a split second. I didn't know why he did that to me, what he must have been thinking in that moment, but I wanted to cry and scream at the same time.

"They're gonna hurt them!" Red screamed as he pointed to the deer that approached the ice birth pods which grew out of the earth.

"We have to leave them," I yelled to Red as I ran after him.

The deer were hungry. And they wouldn't stop until they got their full. Red's unborn siblings were still living there in the ground, growing until they would be ready for this world (which they never would be.) And although it pained me to think about leaving them behind, I knew I couldn't save all of them or stop the deer in time. The only one I knew I could save was Red.

The deer were nearly thirty feet away from him when I got to Red. He was so brave then, standing in front of one of the ice pods, holding his body over it as if that weak frame of his could actually protect it. And I knew that if we waited any longer, the deer would show him how breakable he really was.

I realized it almost too late as the deer in the front of the pack launched off his hind legs toward Red. I panicked as I ripped the rifle off my back and into my hands. With one second to aim, I shot toward the deer a few times, hoping that at least one of the bullets hit them. But I missed, and I almost wanted to drop the rifle and run as I saw that all five of the deer were still alive.

"Red, come on!" I screamed.

The deer were disoriented for a moment, and I took that chance to lunge forward and grab Red by the arm. I dragged him away as he clung to the pod, but eventually he picked up his feet to run beside me. I trusted him to rely on his footing as I reloaded the rifle and prepared to shoot again. We were going to get to that tower … we were so close that I almost knew it was impossible not to make it. But I had a shot loaded, just in case.

Red was running beside me when we were just a few yards away from the door. And then suddenly … he was not. I heard his body thump against the ground as he tripped over a rock. And my body felt so heavy then that it took all of my strength to pull my arms in the air and aim my rifle at the incoming deer.

I shot once …. twice … three times in the air, only catching glimpses of the torn brown pelts and the branching antlers flashing before me. In the silence, when I thought the bullets would have been enough … I realized I was wrong. Two deer had fallen, but three still stood. They pulled Red off the ground before I could. And he screeched as they plucked him in the air and slammed him back to the frozen earth again.

"No," I whispered in a panic as I scrambled backward and reloaded the rifle with my shaky hands.

But it was too late. Red's body was a crumpled ball on the ground as two of the deer stomped on him, causing spurts of blood to spew out of his mouth. I was so shocked by what I was seeing, so stilled that I couldn't get my hands to work.

I just watched as two more bit onto whatever was left of his hands and ripped them apart. And then the frenzy began. They feasted, and I couldn't do anything to stop it.

"Please … stop!" Red panicked in a loud, shrill voice as the cries clouded his throat.

And that was the last I heard of Red. His body was only a pile. I hated that I just watched, that I didn't keep shooting to try and stop the deer, that I didn't do something else to save Red. But when I saw what happened to him, all I could remember is that it would happen to me if I didn't get the hell into that tower.

While the deer were still occupied with their … feast, I turned and pushed myself toward the door of the tower. Red was right, it wasn't locked. The front door swung open without a hitch. I held my rifle in the air, expecting anything to greet me there. But there was no life there in the contents of the first room. I turned to face the door quickly as I found the large pin that locked it shut. Stanly didn't lock the elves out, but he could have. I was thankful for that flat piece of wood because it saved me from having to face the deer again.

I tried to catch my breath as I surveyed the room I was in. As I got a good look around, I was beginning to think that it was almost better to be back outside. The landing of the tower was just a big room, empty of all furniture or things of value. But it was full in so many other ways. Limp bodies of elves lay scattered and parsed to pieces in sorted piles on the floor. Gift boxes sat wide open next to chunks of bloodied snow. And I vomited in the corner as I looked at the harvest in front of me.

I found the stairs to my right, and I wasn't sure if I could wait to go up in case the noises of my gun had warned Stanly that there was an intruder in his tower. But then I heard the screams, echoing from the top of the stairs, too far away to determine if they were real or part of my imagination. I remembered what Red said … follow the screams. Red … I wished he was still there. I wished he wasn't so brave like he had been. I wished I could have saved him. It was like I had trained my whole life for this moment because I had years of practice following screams. I thought maybe this would be the last time I would have to.

I nearly slipped on the first step as I stumbled up the stairs. The packed snow on the bottom of my boots ruined the traction. But I didn't have time to scrape the snow off, didn't want to think about waiting any longer for the deer to tear at the door, with bits of Red hanging out of their jaws. So I hurried, hoping that my next step wouldn't cause me to tumble down the whole flight. I was running away from one terror and toward another. I wasn't counting the steps as I climbed. I was counting all the snow gifts I had ever held, the rifle shots that couldn't save Red, and all the screams I heard at night, the ones that sounded familiar to the ones that echoed even louder from the top of the staircase now.

When I got to the top of the stairs, ragged breaths riddling my chest because I had never climbed so fast before, I saw some things that I will never be able to un-see, heard some things that still ring through my ears today.

The old man I could only assume to be Stanly stood with his back facing the stairs. And I remembered what Red said about him being deaf. He didn't even know I was there, couldn't even hear me walking up the stairs. So I stood for a moment and took in the scene, watching what he was doing but immediately regretting it.

A group of seven elves stood in a semi-circle around him, shivering, squealing, panicking, and crying out for help. But Stanly couldn't hear their cries.

Blood splattered onto the floor, thick and wet, wet like snails that I hated so much. And the screams were so loud that I forgot they existed, the deafness having taken over me, the strangeness of the image making me forget my senses. Stanly was sorting the heap of body parts that he held in both hands. I remember the vibration against my feet, crawling through my tired legs. The fingers, the ears, the tongues, and even eyes, plopped into their respective buckets—a jolting sensation that will never be parted from my memory.

And the man with his back to me, the one who held the knife in his claw like hand, he was weak and gangly. His body looked sick like a tree that had lost all its leaves with roots decaying, limbs snapping and breaking. He wasn't a strong, brave man who posed any real threat to me or the village. He was just an old man with scraggly grey hair and a crooked spine who hid away and preyed on the weak. And in the real world without the elves to do his bidding, I knew he would have been the prey.

I don't know why he did it, or what sort of thrill he got out of doing what he did to the elves and my people. But that's the thing … I didn't need to know. The only important question was answered. Stanly was the one who was sending the snow gifts to the kids, the ones I was supposed to protect. He was the one who made Nancy's cheeks stained with tears, the one who taught Tommy to fear the one day that *should* be celebrated. He was the one who turned Christmas bad. And I knew as the blood that spewed from the faces and fingers of the elves soaked into his pants, that's all he wanted.

The battered elves stopped screaming as I shot Stanly in the back of the head with my rifle. Silence penetrated the air. He fluttered to the ground in a panic, arm flailing, legs jerking, and then nothing … dead. It was the first time I killed a man, and I was terrified how easy it actually was. I wondered if that was why Stanly did what he did, because it was so easy. The thick puddle of blood that oozed out from his hair and crawled around his body was the last I hoped to see for a lifetime.

"You saved us! Thank you …" one of the elves cried as he gathered around with his brothers and sisters and helped them bind their wounds.

The room was busy with tools, crates, and tables with oddly shaped boxes stacked on top. There was a window at the back of the room, and I ran toward it to look outside. The deer were already gone, and the ice pods that once held all the unborn elves were empty, all holding a small pool of blood. I breathed quickly for a moment, trying to gather my senses as I realized none of the innocent children down there could have been saved. The only thing that comforted me was that I knew it was unlikely I'd see the deer again after that.

"Where do you put the presents you took from the villages?" I asked as I walked back to the elves.

I kicked Stanly's body once for good measure, wishing that Red could see it and rejoice in his fall. An elf who was taller than the rest pointed to the other side of the room, behind the dark wood benches, to a door that sat cracked open. I hurried around the maze of crates as I ran to the door. On the other side of the door, there was a stack of gifts, some I was sure came from other villages.

I left the tower that day with a sled full of gifts and a piece of paper with directions on it. The elves hugged me goodbye and thanked me again for my help, but I knew it wouldn't be the last time I would see them. The Barons would hear about what happened. And although it would be a difficult thing to explain, once they had met the elves and seen what happened to them, they would have to help them.

It was Christmas Eve when I trekked back through the tundra with the sled, holding onto hope that I wouldn't encounter the deer again. I stopped a few times on the way, letting the tears fall onto my bare neck as I thought about all I had seen on that long day, as I remembered that Red was wearing my scarf when he died.

It was barely dark when I returned to the village, still recovering from my trek across the snowy tundra. I knew I needed to call a town meeting, but I had one thing I wanted to do first. I knocked on Nancy's door, hoping that I didn't wake her, but knowing that what I had to say was so much more important than her sleep.

"Nick?" she said as she opened the door. "We've been worried sick about you. Where were you?" she asked as she flung her arms around me and embraced me in a hug.

"I was making sure that Tommy had something to open this year," I said as I walked into her house and handed Tommy a gift wrapped in green and blue paper.

"Are you sure it's safe?" she asked reluctantly as Tommy held the large gift in his arms.

"I'm sure," I said as I grabbed her hand.

She nodded as Tommy sat on the floor and opened the present. There was a toy wagon inside, with miniature horses that attached to the front. He immediately took to playing with it on the colorful rug that was spread across the floor.

"What did you do?" Nancy asked with only half a smile as if she wasn't sure if it was safe to be happy yet.

"I did what I had to do to get Christmas back," I said as I turned toward the door. "Now do you want to help hand out the rest of the presents?"

Nancy couldn't hide her smile as she stood with me in the town center and handed each member of the village a gift. And instead of taking them home and opening them the next morning, we all opened them together in the town center. The first few people were reluctant until they opened their gifts and saw real presents inside. They didn't understand how I came across them, and they didn't really need to know. I just told them I took care of everything, that I made it to where we could start enjoying Christmas again.

"I'm sorry," I said to Nancy as the shrill noises of the children playing drowned out my voice.

"Why would you be? You saved Christmas!" she exclaimed as she hugged me again.

But this time, I didn't let her pull away so quickly. Under the stars and the light snow fall, I kept Nancy Reed close to me and looked into her eyes that were full of hope again.

"I'm sorry that your holiday was scary. And I'm sorry that the gift I got you might not be enough to make you forget about it all," I said reluctantly.

"You got me a gift?" she asked with a smile.

"Well, it's more of a question," I said as I held her hand.

"What is it?" she asked with a small hint of worry.

"I know I could never replace him … but will you let me be Tommy's father? And I mean … will you be my wife?" I spat the words out so quickly that I wasn't sure she heard me.

But she did hear me. And she kissed me then, the warmth of her lips thawing my face, and I didn't have to ask her to know that she meant yes.

That was the last year of the snow gifts and haunted Christmas. The Barons were terrified by what they found at the north tower. The only thing they could do was offer the elves a means of living since they had been abandoned by the death of their abusive guardian.

So, from then on, the elves lived in the Charity building. They made toys for themselves, so they could explore what it was like to be a child for once. And while some recovered from their wounds and trauma, the rest helped us make Christmas gifts for all the villages each year. And finally, after the years of terror and darkness, we celebrated Christmas how it was always meant to be, in happiness.

The village was much better off after that. After many meetings with the Barons and all of the villagers, we decided to build a fence around our village, one that would keep the deer and other awful things out. We were determined to keep our village happy. And although I'm still haunted sometimes by the snow gifts and the things that happened that one Christmas Eve, the memories began to fade over time and became less real.

Years later, when Tommy was a teenager and Nancy and I had two boys of our own together, they came up with a question that couldn't remain unanswered. *Who was Stanly?* They asked as if they'd uncovered a bit of lost history that we meant to forget. Other kids were asking the same thing, probably passing down the name they heard as a whisper from older stories that refused to die. Some parents told their kids the truth. They thought it was only fair. But I couldn't …

Stanly used his power to make us afraid. But we weren't afraid anymore, and we were determined not to lose that hope. But the kids were curious, and we knew that their questions couldn't remained un-answered forever.

"Oh … you mean Santa," I finally said to our son, Avery, who looked at me with wide eyes like Tommy once did.

"Santa?" our other son, Remus, asked.

"Yeah. You mean Santa. He's the jolly old man who works with the elves in the Charity House," I said as I sat with my son on the rug by the fireplace.

"He lives with the elves?" Avery asked.

"Yeah, and he helps them make presents for you each year for Christmas," I smiled as I pulled Remus into my arms.

"What does he look like?" Avery asked in excitement as if I was sharing a secret with him.

"He has a round belly," Nancy began as she sat in her rocking chair and worked on her quilt. "And a thick white beard," she added with a smile.

"White like the snow?" Remus asked.

"Yeah … and he wears a thick red and white coat, so he can stay warm while he's outside," Tommy added as he stacked wood in the fire place.

"Why does he go outside?" Avery asked.

"So he can deliver the gifts to us Christmas Eve," I said.

"But I thought the Charity does that …" Remus recalled.

"They do, but he helps them. He carries the heavy gifts on his sled," I explained to the boys.

"Oh … will we ever see Santa?" Remus asked eagerly as Tommy sat next to him on the floor with a cup of hot cider in his hands.

"Maybe if you're good you will," I said as I brushed his hair out of his eyes.

So instead of telling our children the truth, the horrors of what we lived, we told them this tale of a jolly fat man who loved cookies and milk. Some parents thought that it wasn't fair to lie to them about our past. But eventually, we all agreed it was best to leave those things behind. This legend was better than the truth. It hid the things we didn't want to remember.

The Yang | *Krystle Kwiatkowski*

Brothers and Sisters,

made of the same blood

forming a bond thicker than water.

Fortunately,

not all bonds break.

Deep and Strong,

sibling bonds can lead

to one rescuing the other.

The Secret Angel | *Krystle Kwiatkowski*

I sat on the front steps of the small-town church. Midnight Mass had just ended, and the place was quiet. There were no cars in the lot, and no one was walking down the sidewalk. Hell, I'm pretty sure the streetlights themselves were ready to quit for the night. They couldn't, though. They had to stay on for the lost souls that wandered the night. That night, the lost soul was me.

I picked at my fingernails. There was no dirt or guck. I just couldn't look at everything anymore. Everything made me think of the past—a past where I was happy and carefree.

The park across from me, for example. In high school, my girlfriends and I would practice our flips for cheerleading. I would always fail the first few tries by either falling to the side or not landing properly. Whenever I got to the tenth attempt, I would finally get it.

And the ice cream parlor behind that. Every year, my younger brother would take me to celebrate the end of the school year, even after high school. We used it as an excuse to hang out. I'd get a sundae and he'd down a chocolate shake or two. Our conversations would go anywhere from laughs to tears. We'd converse about the need to develop a chip that could mute people who were annoying. We'd have deep conversations about our futures—where we were headed, where we wanted to go.

These past two years, though, I never showed up. I couldn't. Not without risking my safety. I wanted to every time the day came around. I fantasized about being there, fantasized about telling my brother the truth of why I pushed him away. That it would hit him like a ton of bricks and he'd take me far away from the life I got myself into. But none of that happened. Instead, I stayed back, scared of what would happen if my husband… ex-husband caught me.

"Well, look what the cat dragged in!"

I snapped my head around. I saw my brother, Marcus, standing on one of the top steps. His grin wide and bright as he looked down at me. He was different since the last time I saw him. His dark hair was buzzcut, he had a bit of stubble, and he was a bit more muscular. Marcus hopped down the steps and plopped himself beside me.

"It's been too long. I've missed ya!"

"Yeah," I said. I kept my eyes down as I continued to pick at my nails. My voice was hoarse and a bit shaky. I managed to get myself to look at him with a smile—a sad smile with frowning eyes, but a smile. Marcus wasn't stupid, though. He was never book smart, nor was he a genius when it came to life, but he knew enough to read people.

He nodded. "How'd you get out?"

I raised my eyebrow. "What?"

"Your marriage. How'd you finally escape?"

I took a deep breath. Tears began to build, but there wasn't enough for them to start falling. "Luck. Pure luck."

"Oh, c'mon," Marcus tsks. "I bet you drop kicked his ass all the way to jail."

I laughed. He always knew how to crack a joke, even in the most serious of times. I cleared my throat as nerves moved their way up to my neck. "I wish it was that badass, but it really wasn't."

"No?"

I shook my head. "He was stuck at work longer than usual. That never happened for he always made sure to be home by 5 o'clock on the dot. No matter what. However, he couldn't get away that night and… something told me to pack up and leave. I took everything I could squeeze into a bag, hopped into the truck, and never looked back."

Marcus exhaled, "I don't know, sounds pretty badass to me."

He nudged me with his arm, I responded with another laugh. It quickly faded, though. Laughing made me feel better, but I didn't want to be pulled out of the darkness. Not yet. I just wanted to feel the sadness rather than avoid it. I wanted to, just for once, stop running away from my feelings. I already did that for years.

I heard Marcus take a deep breath. His demeanor became somber. Like me, he kept his eyes down at his hands, though he looked around, as well—not as hurt by the memories around.

"You okay?"

The tears built up more, but I fought them off. I hated crying. It was worse around other people, especially family. "No."

We were silent, but just for a moment, knowing what we both wanted to say without saying it, understanding each other without so much as a sigh, an unspoken language few people are fortunate to have.

I choked back my emotions in time for him to poke at them again. "You'll be alright," he said knowingly. "I'll make sure of it. We'll all make sure of it."

I laughed to myself. It was so cheesy, the words, but they still comforted me. I guess that's why the words are so overused. They do comfort you when the world feels like it's falling apart. To know that someone has your back can get you through anything. Maybe if I hadn't pushed him away during those years, I would've been saved much sooner. I would've left much sooner, or at least known that I needed to sooner.

"So, why aren't you at home?" Marcus asked me.

I took a deep breath. I had a number of excuses running through my head. Was it because I hoped I could make it to Midnight Mass? No, that wouldn't explain why I was still here long after. Was I waiting for a friend? No, all the people I was friends with… I pushed them away, too.

Marcus told me, "Don't lie."

I took a moment to gather the courage. "I'm scared."

"Scared of what?"

"…to show my face. After everything that has happened."

"There's no reason to be scared. They'll welcome you back with open arms."

"Really?" I looked at him hopefully. I knew he was right, but part of me didn't believe the truth.

"Of course!" Marcus said, "they may give tough love, but they're not assholes. They're not gonna say 'I told you so' over and over again."

The urge to cry became stronger as he spoke. I nodded until the tears became too overwhelming. I put my head in my hands as I broke down. Everything I had been feeling for the past few months came rushing out. I couldn't control it. I wailed as I struggled to breathe.

"I should've listened," I said. "Why didn't I listen?"

I felt Marcus wrap his arms around me. His hug gave me a sense of peace—a sensation of cool air and a calmness that I couldn't describe… still can't describe. My breathing became steady and my crying began to quiet down. He shushed me like a mother does her baby as she rocks them to sleep.

We were quiet. The town was quiet, too, with the exception of a few crickets. Marcus hummed in my ear—a song our mama would sing when we were babies, a song that put us at ease whenever we were upset. Sometimes we were upset about something serious. Other times, it was a stupid, childish thing. No matter what, though, it put my soul at ease. It had been so long since the last time I felt like things will be fine.

Of course, the moment couldn't last forever. Marcus had moved away, and I didn't even notice. My eyes were closed, and I just lost myself in it all. It wasn't until he spoke that I saw he stood at the bottom of the steps, looking at the town.

"Ready to go home?"

I looked at the old clock on the sidewalk. "It's well past midnight. I'm sure they're asleep."

"I'm pretty sure they're eating breakfast." He chuckles, "They stay up even after Midnight Mass is over. The crazies."

I swallowed down the fear that was creeping back up. I cleared my throat and went back to picking my fingernails.

"Don't," Marcus said. He gave me eyes that held sorrow, but also hope. "Don't revert back. You can do this."

I listened to his words and digested them. I was going to believe in them this time. I was gonna believe that he was right, and I could step into the place I was fearing most. He walked down the sidewalk, in the direction of our childhood home. It wasn't long 'til I lost sight of him. I didn't think much of it. After all, Marcus was quite the fast walker.

A minute passed. And another. And another … if I didn't go now, they would surely be asleep. As it is, they were probably sitting down to eat already.

I hopped into my car and drove home. I thought about all the people I might see. Mama and papa for sure. Maybe I'd see my older sister, but she wasn't one for staying up late. For all I know, she could've went to her own home to sleep like a sane person. I would definitely see my younger sister, though. She was still in high school, so of course she'd be with our parents. Marcus, well… I'd be shocked if I didn't see him.

When I arrived, I stared at the house. The lights were on, but I didn't see any movement inside. I took multiple shaky breaths before I stepped out and knocked on the door. I never liked the doorbell, and it'd be a good excuse as to why I didn't come in. After all, how can you hear a knock if you're in a room at the back of the house—which is where the dining room and kitchen are located.

I bounced up and down as I got antsy. My heart raced, and I felt it pounding in my chest. As I tilted my head back and said a little prayer in my head, the door opened. Papa, still in his church clothes, stood in front of me. His expression was that of someone who had seen a ghost. He whispered my name as happiness began to fill him—speechless.

Emotions overwhelmed me, once again. Instead of saying "Hi," I said, "I'm sorry, Papa. You were right."

For the second time that night, I broke down. Papa pulled me in for a hug and I gladly accepted it. He's an overweight man, so it was like hugging a life-size teddy bear. I was quickly pushed away so he could wipe away my tears.

Papa said, "There's no need for that. I'm so happy you're back home. Are you safe? He's not following you, is he?"

"No," I replied, "he is long gone, Papa."

"Good. Now let's go fix you a plate of pancakes and sausages."

He closed the door and we went to the dining room, which was connected to the kitchen. When mama saw me, she nearly dropped the tray of food. She gave me a squeeze tighter than that of a boa constrictor. Following suit was my younger sister and my older sister, who was the only one in her pajamas.

Everyone was beaming at the sight of me. I, on the other hand, was doing my best not to cry.

Mama said, "Well, let's sit down and catch up. We don't want the food getting cold."

We all shared a laugh. I looked around and realized: Marcus isn't here. "Shouldn't we wait for Marcus?" I said.

Silence. Everyone stared at each other, avoiding me. The mood had quickly dropped from what it was. Mama approached me and took my hands into her own. Her voice became soft and gentle, her words were slow and carefully chosen.

"Honey… Marcus died."

My jaw dropped. "What?"

"He was in a car accident a few months ago. He didn't make it, Honey, I'm sorry."

The news hit me hard. I had just seen him—talked to him, even. How could he be dead? I don't know why, but I turned my head to glance at the Christmas tree in the living room. Standing in front of it was Marcus, looking up at the Christmas Angel. I excused myself from everyone and went over to him.

I stood beside him, but instead of looking at the Angel, I looked at him. I talked quietly to ensure no one but Marcus could hear me.

"How?" I asked.

"Doesn't matter. What matters is that you're here."

"Why didn't you tell me?"

"Because that's not what's important right now."

Marcus pointed up to the Christmas Angel. It was passed down to my parents from our grandma. The white dress is slightly yellow, and there was a small hole in the wings. It has been on top of the Christmas tree since long before even mama was born.

Marcus said, "You needed help out, and you needed help getting back home. I love you. You'll be alright, I'm sure of it."

He gave me a smile and I returned it with my own. He said he needed to go, and that I needed to go eat with our family. However, he told me one last thing that I will never forget—words that, to this day, I never let go of.

Marcus told me, "It doesn't matter how far you fall. In time, you can always stand back up. There are always second chances."

Found | *Sam Baker*

I'm lost,
and I'm not sure if lost is okay.
I don't know where I am
or where I'm going.
Is it okay to want to be found?
A thick fog surrounds me,
smothers me.
I don't know what is real.
I need someone to help me,
find me,
show me a place to belong,
teach me *how* to belong.
Because my legs stopped working
long ago.
And I feel like I'm falling …
falling through life
with nothing to hold me in place—
nothing but … you.

Mason

Something was off. I looked down at my watch before seeing the petite brunette walk toward the glass doors. Glancing down, I started to pour steamed eggnog into a to-go cup before watching her again.

She kept brushing strands of hair behind her ear as she walked. Stopping right before the curb, her head glanced back to the parking lot. With a heavy sigh, she adjusted her bag and tripped up on the step.

I quickly refocused, topping the drink—more so making sure she didn't see me see her—before I called out the customer's name. Wishing the customer a 'Happy New Year,' my shoulders relaxed when the glass doors opened and she walked in.

Eyes glued to the ground, her unruly hair crowded her face. Her footsteps were precise and small—no doubt afraid to be betrayed by them again.

I wiped my hands on my apron as I walked over to the register.

We were slow, it was New Year's Eve after all, and five at night. Most people had come in earlier today to get their caffeine fix. Now, most of the city was getting ready for whatever big plans they had.

For me, I was working until seven. I still hadn't decided if I was going to do anything. I had plans—my friends invited me out drinking with them and to watch the ball drop near the lake—but I wasn't feeling it.

"Good evening, Marley," I greeted with a smile.

Marley has been coming to Isabella's Coffee now for as long as I remember. I'm pretty certain she was a customer before I started working here a year ago. She comes in almost every day, except for Tuesday's and Thursday's. She works at night, she says.

Today's a Monday and while it isn't unusual that she's here, she's later than normal. Often she comes in around three, sometimes a quarter after three.

"Hi Mason," her smile is small. It isn't a broad grin that usually illuminates her eyes. She has stunning dark brown eyes. And I don't mean to brag, but I've noticed how they look different when she speaks to someone else. But today? Today, I get the average eyes, except there's a tinge of sadness to them.

"Can I get you the usual?"

For someone who usually only gets bold black coffee, we've developed a great customer/barista relationship. But that's what I loved about my job. We weren't rushing people in or out unless they were in a rush.

"Um," she started taking her wallet out, but it fumbled out of her hands and hit the counter with a clang. "Sure," her sigh was barely noticeable—at least, I imagine, to others. But I caught it.

Shaking my head, I bent my knees slightly to her level, catching her eyes with my own. Quickly, she looked down.

"How about something different? Something comfortable? I bet it's freezing out."

I nodded toward her parka and then glanced outside to the snow-covered ground. It wasn't snowing today—and hopefully, wouldn't—but it was still close to zero.

She gave me a measly smile before looking up at the menu.

Marley only ever got a soy latte with cinnamon sprinkled on top when she treated herself to a latte. But those were often just on Sunday's.

"Can I surprise you?"

If I wasn't mistaken, I saw a glimmer of light in her eyes.

She nodded.

"How about you go settle down and I'll bring it over?" She started searching through her wallet. "My treat."

Marley was about to argue with me but mumbled out a soft thank you before heading toward the open cafe.

She often sat up front and center, where the light poured through the coffee shop, at a table where she could plug her laptop into an outlet. She typed away for hours some days. But sometimes Marley would just stare out the window, letting the screen grow black, sipping her coffee as she watched others walk past on the sidewalk.

Today she passed her favorite table. Instead, she took a seat by the fireplace we had, in our quieter section.

I immediately pulled the soy milk out of the fridge below me and started working on a latte. I made her my favorite comfort drink—a salted caramel mocha—fixing it with all the toppings sans whipped cream.

Right before I carried the mug over to her, I eyed the pastry case. Seeing the lonesome chocolate croissant, I made the decision to heat one up before I carried both over to her. She sat barely unpacked, just watching the flickers of the fire. They were fake, of course, an electric fireplace, but I was mesmerized by them quite often.

"Hey," I said softly, afraid to scare her.

Regardless, she jumped, looking over at me.

Her entire stature was off. Her shoulders caved in as she relaxed—only slightly—in front of me.

I placed the drink and pastry on the table. She never ate here, so I was hoping I chose well.

"Thank you, Mason." She tried, I saw the effort that went into her bright smile, but it was lost somewhere deep within her.

Tentatively, glancing over at the door, I chose to take a seat across from her.

"Everything okay today?"

Leaning over, she took the mug in her hands, bringing the drink up to her lips. Her eyes watched mine, the wheels in her mind going a mile a minute. As she opened her mouth, I heard the glass doors open and a rush of people chattering in.

"Rain check?" I smiled, lifting my brow slightly.

With a soft nod, she looked back at the fireplace, but she closed her eyes.

It took everything in me to stand and force my steps back to the bar. Her sunken frame wasn't lost on me nor was her deep breath. There wasn't time to make sure her eyes opened before the teenagers grew impatient.

Marley Mae

I shouldn't have come here. I should have just stayed home, safely in my bedroom. One, it wouldn't feel like I was lying to my friends who invited me out tonight. And two? Mason. He doesn't know me, so why does it feel like he does?

Sure, I see him almost every day—some days he doesn't work when I'm here—he does deserve a day off, but those one to two … okay, maybe five-minute conversations? Is that enough for a friendship?

He's already asked the question that none of my friends have. They did a while back when it was really bad. But lately? Lately, no one asks anymore because no one cares.

They shouldn't have to. I should be able to talk to them, bring up what's going on, explain why I am the way I am.

But I can't.

It's not that I don't want to … okay well, maybe that's part of the reason. But really, it's because I don't know why I am this way. I'm trying. I really am. However, I'm starting to gather that those around me don't believe me anymore or they do, but they can't be bothered to care.

I get it.

It just seems like I'll never get better.

And some days I question whether that's true.

This drink helps though. So does the fire … and seeing the snow from a distance. Silly, isn't it? This warm beverage in a place that isn't my home brings me comfort. How materialistic. Or maybe, it's good that small things can bring comfort. A sense of peace in the chaos of my mind.

Mason walked past, rag in hand, shooting me a smile. I feel the blood beneath the surface of my skin start to crawl as my little hairs stand up. This isn't what I need. The last thing I need is him making a move on me, today of all days.

This isn't … this wasn't some romantic 'I fell in love with my barista' story. I refuse to let it be that. Besides, love? I wasn't someone to love. I could hardly love myself.

I came here because this shop makes me feel at home. This was my sanctuary.

Mason, so help me, don't ruin this.

I need to do something. I brought my book, my book will help. Just dive into someone else's life for a while, right? Self-care … everyone always preaches about self-care, including myself. But really, what did that mean?

What brings you comfort, Marley? Go through the checklist.

Coffee? Check. Favorite sweater? I looked down and smiled at my NASA sweatshirt, check. Fireplace? Check. Good book? Check.

I could do this. I could stay.

Stay, Marley.

Taking a long sip from my latte, I savored the flavor in my mouth, took a deep breath through my nose, and swallowed as I breathed out.

No one else was hanging out here except for me and Mason … and well, another worker who I could overhear Mason speaking to.

The big crowd of rowdy teenagers left with their drinks. Mason was busy the entire time, with a steady flow of people coming in and leaving—but that was good. That meant he couldn't come and ask me the one thing I needed someone to ask, but the exact thing I never wanted to answer.

Was I okay?

Mason

She had a book placed on the table before her, but never once opened it. Marley picked it up, turned it over in her hands, and then placed it back down.

The pastry was gone, but not before she ate it slowly, catching each and every crumb as she scanned the cafe each time something dropped. She had a skill for making the latte last for quite some time. It was most likely cold by the time she finished it.

It was nearing closing time—myself and my co-worker were almost finished with cleaning up the store, and Marley was still here.

Since I was the shift supervisor on duty, I asked my co-worker to finish up the tasks and I made my way back to Marley.

She instantly sat rigid, glancing over at me.

"S-sorry, you guys must be closing for the holiday." She started to grab her book, but I placed my hand on hers, lowering the book back to the table.

"No rush." I immediately took my hand off hers though. Her body recoiled into the chair. I was already failing. "Do you, um, do you have plans for tonight?"

She took a few moments to answer, twisting the ring on her right hand with her thumb. Her left hand ran through the waves in her hair.

"No, I don't care for New Year's."

"What?" I exclaimed, letting out a soft laugh. "It's such a great holiday for fresh beginnings."

I was a hypocrite, I know. But how could someone as amazing as she seemed to be, not love the idea of new beginnings and resolutions?

"It's bullshit." She let out before her cheeks grew rosy.

I hid my bulging eyes, letting a smile appear instead.

"Bullshit because why wait—"

"You can change whenever you please. Why wait until January to do so? You're just putting it off, which means you aren't ready for a change. And okay, that's fine. You need to be ready in order to succeed, but just be honest with yourself!" She rushed out, interrupting me.

I sat back in the comfy chair, amused at this girl before me.

I could see her growing discomfort and half expected her to apologize for her outburst, but she didn't. Instead, she grabbed her book and stuffed it back in her bag.

"Marley?" She glanced up. "Would you like to not celebrate New Year's Eve with me?"

Her immediate response was almost a no. I could see it on the tip of her tongue. Her hand grew white as she gripped her backpack.

"I-I'm sorry." I blurted. "That was … I uh, I just … I canceled on my friends tonight because I didn't want to celebrate and well, I'm sort of thinking it might be nice to do something low key. No drunks, no expectations, just as friends?"

I chose to ignore the fake smile that graced her lips as she agreed. She wasn't comfortable. She didn't want to do this. But I was almost a hundred percent certain it wasn't because she didn't trust me—she had other reasons.

Marley Mae

I'm a people pleaser. I hate saying no, so that's exactly why I'm in the position I'm in. I could have come up with an excuse. I could have just plainly said no, I don't think he would have been offended—well it shouldn't matter if he was offended because it's my life. But no, I want to make sure he has a good night, so I'd go along, despite how I feel.

It's gotten me in bad positions before. Really bad situations, but despite that, I continue to do so. It's almost as if I'm trying to make myself worse. Like I'm just asking the universe to fuck me over in every way it can. Life becomes easier to live that way, ironically. Because then there's a reason.

Really, that's the most important.

So I somehow find myself following Mason down the street. Some of the businesses have closed up shop for the night, some never even opened. But there's a great restaurant on the promenade that overlooks the lake that we walk to. I've been a few times with my friends, mostly on birthdays, but this suddenly seems more like a date.

My palms grew clammy despite my frozen fingertips and my pace slows as I create a gap between us walking.

Mason looked behind him, stopping his feet, waiting for me to catch up.

Damn him.

He doesn't continue though. His eyes just search mine, calling my name when I walk past him for me to stop. So I do.

I'm a fucking puppet sometimes.

"What's your favorite thing in the world?"

A laugh filters through the walls I've been putting up.

"What?"

"Your favorite thing? I uh, I suddenly don't feel like sitting down and eating."

"You aren't hungry?"

"Well … okay, maybe I do want to eat. But this seems fancy, right? And it's New Year's Eve and there's a lot that goes with that, so um," he clears his throat, glancing around the promenade.

Every place here is fancy. It's the Mackenzie Promenade.

"What don't you want to do?" He questioned, suddenly.

Out of nowhere, it felt like we were the only two people milling around. And maybe we were. Because it was freezing, and everyone was gathering with their friends—indoors—where reservations were already placed. Looking up ahead, it seems like we might not even be able to go to the restaurant because it's packed.

I really didn't want to be here standing outside. But, if I was being honest with myself, I did enjoy his company.

It was new and fresh. I could be who I wanted to be and not what my friends expected. He invited me out even seeing me at my worst he's seen.

"I don't want to be around people." The words fluttered through my lips.

Shit, Marley. That sounds like you actually want to be alone with him … like more than a friend.

I swiveled on my foot and immediately started walking back toward my car. We hadn't walked that far. I could do it—brace the cold a little longer.

I felt my stomach bubbling up my throat. I knew I wouldn't get sick, but it would cause me discomfort until I was out of this place, until I was safely wrapped in my comforter in my bedroom. Why did I leave in the first place? It was a mistake.

Stupid self-care!

"Marley?" His words were so soft. He was afraid. He wasn't here to hurt me or manipulate me. And he's never, in the entire time I've known him, hit on me or suggest that he'd be inappropriate.

Of course, I've watched his mannerisms numerous times. On good days, I loved watching his interactions with customers. And on bad days? Bad days I was envious of his ways.

But why me? Why ditch his friends and hang out with little 'ol me?

I stopped walking, but I didn't turn around.

"Marley, I'm sorry. I … I know something is going on today and I just want to help. I just, I don't know." He shoved his hands further into his jacket as I turned toward him. "Look, why don't we get take out and go back to Isabella's? Talk? Just hang out? Away from people?"

"I don't want to be around people, but I prefer to be near people. I uh—"

Panic consumed his face. I didn't have to finish my sentence. He understood, which was enough to know it was safe. Mason didn't try and argue his point like others would, instead, a smile appeared, and he held up his finger.

He walked a few steps away, dialed a phone number and waited. Eventually, he started talking in whispers. I could pick up Isabella's Coffee, but that was it.

Mason had a grin on his face when he came back to me.

"How about we hang out at Isabella's on the promenade? We can people watch from the windows, have a warm drink, and eat some food?"

I raised a brow, about to argue. He was clever.

"I just called the owner, he told me as long as it was in top shape for the workers when they reopened, then we were good. He trusts me. Perks of being a supervisor."

His wink was subtle, and I even managed to crack a smile.

"Okay," I agreed quietly, but my insides were turning. It wasn't excitement. I didn't know excitement at the moment, but there would be a momentary crack where he could get through if he wanted to … *if* I wanted him to.

The two of us set off a few storefronts down, past the crowded restaurant and right next door where Isabella's Coffee was. I only ever went to this one with friends; I liked the other one to work in because it was quieter.

But this one, with just the two of us, would surely be quiet. Aside from the outside noise that'd be muffled by the glass windows, it was the perfect place to people watch, as now everyone was dressed to the nines. Before we knew it, they'd be hobbling home.

"Pizza?" Mason suggested.

I nodded, and he took it upon himself to place an order on his phone. While doing so, he went behind the bar and started messing around. I usually hated when people ordered for me, especially when they didn't even ask what I generally liked, but tonight, tonight I couldn't really make decisions. It was nice he was making the decisions.

But I couldn't let it continue like this. What if he thought that's who I was? What if this new impression I was making was the wrong one because I was making the impression that I didn't care to make decisions for myself?

I jumped as a hand gripped my shoulder.

"Sorry!" He squeaked. "Sorry, I knew you were in a trace. Uh … that was stupid. I, uh, I apologize." His rambling was cute.

I shook my head and shimmied off my jacket that I still had on.

"You're okay."

The warm air wasn't making me brave. I had more confidence in the freezing temperatures, desperate to get into a new situation. But while the warmth brought comfort, it also had me closing off.

How could this be smart? Neither of us knew anything about each other and I was not in the place to make new friends.

"Wanna tell me what's wrong?"

But how did he know? We barely conversed.

"I'm fine. When will the pizza be here?"

"Twenty minutes. And you're not fine. It's okay if you don't want to talk, but I know you well enough to know that something is wrong."

"How?" I didn't want to know. Not really. But then I did. I was just with my best friend earlier who had no idea. How could he?

"Don't run off?" It wasn't a joke. He seemed genuinely afraid that I'd leave him. A slight nod had him sitting down across from me at the table. "First off, you usually have a conversation with me." A raise of the brow had him clarifying. "Not like now. But back when you came into the shop. We didn't talk. I always look forward to you coming in."

He did? I looked forward to seeing him too. I often avoided the days I knew he wouldn't be there. He was my comfort in the shop. If he wasn't there, I'd end up back home.

"You usually come in around three too. Today you were late, but maybe it's because of the holiday?"

I didn't answer him. But he knew an awful lot about me and my schedule. I wasn't sure if I should be comforted or overwhelmed by the thought.

"Your words are soft. You're nervous. Uncomfortable even? Afraid?" Gosh, this boy needed to stop reading into everything I did. Correction: this was overwhelming information that had me wanting to run for the hills.

But ... I. Was. A. People. Pleaser. I'd sit here in agony before rushing off in case I disappointed him.

I hated myself sometimes ... *a lot* of the time.

"I noticed you almost turned around and you almost didn't come into the shop today at all."

He saw me before I even got into the shop? Was I making a mistake? I shouldn't be alone with this guy. Surely this was all a ploy to murder me.

But ... I let out a sigh. I almost turned away because I didn't see him at first. And then I did and he gave me that extra encouragement to go in.

"I'm glad you did. I'm glad I saw you today. And I'm glad ... I'm glad that you're letting me spend New Year's with you. It's really an honor."

"An honor?" I choked.

Out of all the information he gave, *that's* what I chose to focus on?

He nodded, seemingly at ease with it all.

"Yeah, Marley. I've wanted to get to know you for quite some time, but I never knew how to ask you to hang out."

I chose this moment to look out the window, pressing my fingertips against the glass, trying to find some cool air to lower the temperature of my face.

"If you don't want to talk about whatever is going on—judgment free zone, I'll add—then I want to make sure you have a really great time tonight. Maybe take the focus off of what's going on in your head?"

"What do you have in mind?"

It was clear that this wasn't thought out because his face dropped. He had been hoping for me to open up.

I let out a genuine laugh. He was just trying so hard. My heart started to feel a little lighter.

"Marley?" His words were almost a whisper.

The tension in the air grew thick, and I found myself pressing my palm against the window instead of my fingertips, but I couldn't break eye contact. Why couldn't I break eye contact with him?

"You should laugh more. It's beautiful."

I felt the weight in my shoulders slacken as I visibly lost strength to hold them up. In an instant, I was up and out of my seat. A breath in and out and I'd show him a new side of me. I couldn't—I wouldn't let him in.

"You know what I've always wanted to do?" My voice was an octave higher and almost back to normal.

I can play this game.

His shock was evident as he turned in his chair to watch me.

"What's that, Marley?"

"I've always wanted to learn how to make a latte."

Mason studied me and I turned away from his stare, walking toward the bar. I don't know what overcame me. It was a false confidence I was sure. It happened sometimes.

"You've come to the right person then." He was catching up to me, following behind the bar.

I could feel his mood starting to shift, becoming okay with what was happening. If one can be okay? This boy was not an idiot.

Mason

I've been making lattes for five years. It's a skill I've mastered. But teaching Marley? That was a skill within itself. She was terrible. It was good she stuck with writing … well, at least, I hoped she was a good writer.

We even paused to get the pizza before going back to learning. She was determined to make a great latte for herself and I was determined to not eat cold pizza … mainly because I *was* actually starving.

"Wait!" She exclaimed.

She was giggling as her soy milk foamed—I was certain all the milk we used would be taken out of my paycheck—and she pushed me away when I came to see.

"No, no. I think I understand."

Aside from the fact that her mug didn't even have espresso in it yet, I wasn't sure she *did* understand.

"Go set up the pizza, I'm going to make you a drink this time."

"So sure of yourself?" I was already heading out into the lobby when she flashed me that bright smile I loved.

"Yup."

She flipped a switch so fast. I wouldn't question her on it. I hoped it was genuine, but I was almost certain she had just suppressed her emotions further.

"Hey, how'd you like to eat by the fire?"

She nodded, her focus on the drink in front of her, but a smile was there.

I rushed to the back room to flip on the electric fireplace and then grabbed some plastic plates and napkins before bringing them to the back of the cafe. This shop had the fireplace near the reading nook. So now we were shielded from the public eye … but I think she was okay with that. I hoped she knew I wouldn't try anything.

By the time that I had pizza on each plate, she was walking slow and steady with a latte in each hand.

"This may be the hardest thing I've ever done." Her voice was comical as she tried not to move a centimeter from her position. "Don't!" She yelled through her lips as I tried to come and help.

I knew from prior experience, that it often caused drinks to slip and fall when others assume you've taken hold.

I held up my hands and went to take a seat. She placed the mugs ever so softly on the coffee table we had before sitting down.

"Whoa. I'm impressed you do that for a living. People need to give baristas more credit."

I smiled at that. We were often under-appreciated. But at Isabella's, we had a great customer base that genuinely liked us and thought we were hard workers mostly because it wasn't a corporation.

I took a hold of my mug and she did with hers. If I wasn't mistaken, she may have been joking around about not knowing how to make a latte, because this was pretty flawless.

I invisibly tapped my mug against hers before taking a sip—toffee nut … a good 'ol favorite.

"This is delicious, Marley."

"Thanks, Mason." She seemed lighter, happier even.

✳✳✳

"Do you ever wonder how someone so close to you may not be able to notice things that a stranger could?"

We were sitting in silence, enjoying our lattes and the fire after we had a few slices of pizza. Honestly, I wasn't even pressing a conversation because after a long shift, this was what I wanted … needed even.

"What do you mean?"

"Like, your best friend … how could it be possible that they don't pick up on the slight shifts when like, someone like you could?"

"Are we talking real life or hypothetical?"

She wouldn't look at me but I feared for each word that left my lips.

"Real."

I could barely hear the word.

"Sometimes we are too close to the situation. Sometimes … we feel when we are that close, if something were wrong, our friend would mention it, and we shouldn't have to pick up on it? Essentially, in an ideal world, best friends don't hide things."

"But they do."

"They do," I agreed, nodding.

I placed my mug on the coffee table and turned toward her. But she scrunched further up into her chair—her boots had been removed right before we ate. She was anxiously at ease.

"We don't tell those closest to us because we don't want to be a burden. We don't tell *anyone* because we don't want to be a burden. But mostly … we don't tell our best friends because we don't want them to feel helpless or feel like a disappointment."

She locked eyes with me. I never turned the house lights on, so we were sitting in dim light with just the flicker of the fire. It made her eyes seem more distressed than before.

Marley needed to speak. She had something to say but the words refused to escape her lips. I had been there … one too many times to date. But I couldn't be certain we were talking about similar situations.

"Marley?" I loved the way her name rolled off my tongue. "You aren't a disappointment. And I'm almost certain your closest friends wouldn't think so either. But, if you'd rather discuss it with me and never speak of it again, I'm happy to listen."

Marley Mae

You'd think he was offering me the perfect package. But he wasn't. Mason didn't know that he was the safe haven in Isabella's. He didn't realize that I needed him to be there, the same as always starting on the second of January, (mainly because tomorrow they were closed). I needed that constant in my life because that routine kept me alive and breathing— kept me living. It was as simple as that.

"You're too close to the situation," I mumbled, drinking the last of my lukewarm latte.

I was certain I'd never sleep tonight.

"How?" He whispered, leaning forward, elbows on his thighs.

"I need things a certain way and I need Isabella's to remain that way."

He nodded and was silent.

We could continue in this silence, let the New Year roll in and go our separate ways, pretend none of this happened. I'd go back to Marley Mae, the girl who gets a bold coffee at three in the afternoon every day. And he'd go back to just Mason, the supervisor of Isabella's Coffee, the guy who lifts my heavy heart without even knowing.

"I have a favorite place," he started and I looked up and over at him. "It's in Lake Mackenzie park, off a beaten path of one of the trails. I go there often to be alone, especially now after a long day at work. It's about a fifteen-minute walk from the main entrance, but I've been known to walk all the way there and to turn directly back around if anyone is in seeing distance." My breath stopped in my throat and I turned ever so slightly toward him.

"It's my place to be alone and I don't want to be judged or have that silence interrupted. I know it's silly. I know that the people who are around aren't judging me. They probably don't even know I'm there. It's becoming a more populated area though, and I've had to learn how to force myself to stay, how to find peace in my once perfect place. It isn't easy every day. There are still days that I turn around and go home more frustrated than when I arrived. But I'm trying."

He twisted his fingers together in his lap. His eyes glanced up at the ceiling and he took a deep breath in. I counted seven seconds in, a four-second pause, and seven seconds out.

We had a connection.

This funny, outgoing, ray of sunshine that I always saw him as at work wasn't who was sitting in front of me.

"Marley?" I gave him a slight nod to continue. "I don't know what you're going through or what you have gone through. I may be way off course with what I'm saying and under no circumstances do you need to continue the conversation if you don't want, okay? But there's something I'd like to share with you."

"Okay," I breathed.

My hands were curled in the sleeves of my sweater and pressed tightly against my stomach and thighs. I was curled in a ball in front of a boy I barely knew, yet I felt we were about to share a connection no one else could.

"I suffer from depression and anxiety. I have for many years now. I'm actually on medication to regulate it. In asking for help, two things happened: I lost some friends, but I gained even stronger friends too. Those who walked away truly were never my friends, I recognize that despite how difficult it was to see them leave in my darkest time. But what am I left with? I'm left with those I know I can be honest with. My closest friends know how to make me feel better, how to take my mind off of things, or just listen when I need them to. They don't ask me when I'll get better or to just shake off the feeling. They don't understand fully. They don't always know how to help. But they do know how to be there.

"This friend of yours, the one that prompted this conversation, I can't say whether or not they are a good friend. That's up for you to decide. But you should be honest with them if for nothing else, to know who should and shouldn't be in your life. The less negativity surrounding you, the better you are."

I didn't want to cry. I hated that I was crying in front of him. Silently hoping the dim lighting wouldn't reflect my tears was a silly hope when I saw his face change as he finished speaking. He was watching me break down in front of him.

They weren't silent tears as my constant struggle to swallow them down had me heaving and hiccuping.

Said friend shouldn't be in my life, and I knew that, but I wouldn't admit it out loud. I wouldn't say it to her face.

I was a people pleaser.

***

I don't know how much time passed as he let me ugly cry before him. I had turned back toward the fire, bringing my hands up in front of my face. He had turned toward the fire too, but I could see his glances every few minutes, checking in on me. Mason didn't try to hug me. He didn't try and come over to wipe my tears. He read between the silences. I didn't have to tell him that I was suffering. I didn't have to tell him that it took everything for me to get out of bed this morning—that I started and turned around numerous times before forcing myself into a parking space at Isabella's.

Mason definitely didn't need to know that I was relapsing, that I had already reached my rock bottom and risen above to start falling again, that I was unbelievably infuriated with myself, and that the thought alone made me want to scream and destroy everything.

The noises outside were getting louder—drunker. The New Year's ball, a few blocks away, was set to drop at midnight. With a glance at the outside doors, I could already see crowds of people walking toward it. I wanted to see the ball drop. I missed it every year since they started doing it. But could I pick myself up and walk out into that crowd, into a swarm of strangers with a guy who was still relatively a stranger?

But was Mason a stranger?

"I want to," I hiccuped, wiping my eyes with my sweater, "be happy," I whispered, clearing my throat from the built-up lodged tears.

"Me too," he whispered, just as soft.

My sweater was crusted in black mascara. I couldn't even remember to put on waterproof mascara on my low days.

"I … I know I said things about not believing in resolutions … but that's a lie."

Looking over at him, I saw a small smile on his face.

"I make so many goddamn resolutions. There are post-it notes all throughout my room with things I need to do, want to do, goals for six months, goals for a year, goals for five years. They are just never-ending. But, New Year resolutions seem more daunting. They are always grander ideas. Resolutions that often can't be resolved in a year."

"I agree. We all make such a big deal about them that you have to come up with crazy ideas. And then we're left disappointed."

I nodded, sitting up and looking over at him.

"I know what I want this year."

He imitated my posture.

"I want to see the ball drop tonight. I want to get to know you better. And I want to be happy—work more on my self-care."

His cheeky smile brought butterflies to my stomach. With each word he spoke previously, he was shaving off the walls, little by little.

I wasn't okay.

Maybe I wouldn't be okay tomorrow.

But I'd be okay … soon.

<u>Mason</u>

We cleaned up our cold dinner scraps and washed our mugs, putting the cafe back the way we found it. As we bundled ourselves back up, I knew we had about ten minutes before the ball was going to drop.

I locked the cafe up, sent a quick message to Ben that everything was in working order, and the two of us walked out. Our breaths both sucked in as the cold wind prickled our skin. I could see a visible shiver from Marley's frame beside me. All I wanted was to pull her close to keep her warm—but our territory was still unknown.

So together, side by side—sometimes bumping into each other—we walked toward the ball and the never-ending crowd. Often times, the crowd would be filled with those drinking, but this year, most had a coffee cup in their hands, trying to keep warm—no doubt filled with liquor from a flask.

As we neared an open spot, I saw Ben and his boyfriend, Caden, only a few feet away. They were leaning up against a railing right before you could head down to the lake.

"Hey!" I greeted, hugging Ben and then Caden to me. "This is Marley. Marley, this is Ben, the creator of Isabella's Coffee, and Caden, his boyfriend, and business partner."

The look in Marley's eyes as she met Ben said everything she hadn't told me. She knew Ben's story—it was a part of her ever-growing comfort with Isabella's. She'd been a customer before Ben shared his struggles, but he was the reason she continued to stay.

"It's lovely to meet you," she spoke, shaking Ben's hand. "Thank you for Isabella's." Ben looked over at me with a smile and then pulled Marley into a hug.

I had mentioned that a friend of mine needed some peace and quiet when I asked him about the shop earlier.

"Our doors are always open." He responded.

The crowd grew thicker and I wrapped my arm around Marley's shoulder, pulling her into me. My excuse was I didn't want to lose her, but I didn't miss the blush on her already rosy cheeks.

"Mason?" She spoke, as the crowd started to countdown. Her body turned into mine and she was looking up at me. "You're a part of the reason I come into Isabella's. I don't go in if you aren't there. Just … just know that you've made a difference in my life."

As the crowd cheered 'Happy New Year,' I wrapped my arms tightly around her, resting my head on top of hers.

"Happy New Year, Marley. You are more than enough. And I'm so thankful to be able to start the new year with you."

She lifted her head up, and her brown eyes glistened—tears threatening.

"Happy New Year, Mason."

We didn't know what would happen in the next few minutes, what would happen tomorrow or even the moment she came in a three in the afternoon on January 2nd. But what I did know was at this moment in time, we were able to help each other. So instead of thinking about the future or wishing I had her in the past, I kept her wrapped in my arms—in the present—for as long as I could.

Who am I? | *Sam Baker*

I do not recognize

these footprints in the snow.

Are they mine?

Who am I?

I don't know.

Why am I trekking,

skipping, running all alone?

Why can't I remember

things I should hold close?

I keep going because I'm not afraid,

because curiosity runs through my veins.

I keep searching for a place—

a place to call my home.

Globe-al Warming | *Brittany Evans*

December 14th Day 2 of the snow abyss.

The snowstorm picked up again, the hard flakes slapping against my skin almost knocking me over. I rub my arms as if that'll make up for the fact I don't have any goddamn sleeves. Crunching my hands into fists and the rest of my body into a ball, I realize, this is bullshit. I have to get out of here. Wherever the hell *here* is.

How I've managed to survive this long is beyond me. My body should be made of snow by now. Or at least covered in frostbite. And what about hypothermia? Either way, I need to get out of here. I pull my hat further down over my ears, my scarf wrapped tightly across my face. And yet, I couldn't remember a goddamn sweater, I think.

Nice.

I trudge through the snow with no sense of direction. If I turn to the left, there's snow. The right, snow. Front snow. Back snow.

Every-fucking-where there's snow.

The flakes are too thick to see far ahead at anything resembling civilization or warmth. And that's when it hits me; how'd I even get here?

December 16th Day—get me the hell out of here—**4.**

Well, the good news is, I found a carrot in the snow to satisfy my starving stomach for about five seconds. The bad news is, I'm *still* here. The snow isn't as bad today. I mean, it's *still* snowing, like this place needs more of that stuff. But at least the wind died down a bit. No more blowing at me like it's going to rip me into three pieces.

I haven't figured out where I am yet or how I wound up in this snow hell. But I've started to come up with some pretty good theories. Now hear me out, what if I was kidnapped? Maybe a gang of some sort robbed me, knocked me unconscious and tossed me from a helicopter into this snow land. The knocking me unconscious could explain why I have no memory of how I even got here.

December 19th Day 7: a goddamn week of this.

So, after my existential crisis, I realized I have no idea who the fuck I am--God, I don't even know my own name for crying out loud—I decided; you know what, it doesn't matter. It doesn't matter if I can't get out of here anyway. Sure, I spent the last three days of my life screaming, crying, and kicking snow like that'll get rid of it. But I'm *fine*. I'm sure I have a family worried sick about me and once I see them I'll remember them and we can all laugh about this endeavour. I just can't lose hope. I bet they're out here looking for me too.

Speaking of hope, I see something. No. *Someone.* A person.

Oh. My. God.

Yes, finally another living creature besides me in this wasteland of snow. I can't kick through the snow fast enough as I approach the figure in the distance.

As I come closer to the silhouette my excitement melts away.

I am, in fact, screwed.

It's not a person. It's not even an animal. It's a fucking pole. The kind that looks like the end of a candy cane stuck in the ground.

Great. Fantastic. That sure is helpful.

In frustration, I pound my forehead against the pole repeatedly until my eye catches something. Down the hill, there's a house. A town. And their lights are on. Civilization, at last. Or so I think.

December 20th Day 8 and hopefully the last day of this.

It may have taken a whole *fucking* day to reach the bottom of that hill. Especially after a snowstorm that knocked me back at least fifteen feet. And after, I fell and rolled part of the way down only to get stuck. I made it. I'm here at last.

The snow has been plowed through the small village to reveal a stone path. Only a few snowflakes rest on its rocky trail. There are only four houses in this place but fuck, who cares, I'm not picky. It still means there's life here. The houses are brown with brown picket fences to match. Thick icicles hang from the triangular roofs. Green Christmas wreaths hang from the door and windows. But the best part of this perfect looking town is that there's light on the other side of those *beautiful* windows.

I walk up to the closest house and knock on the door. Maybe I'm from this village. Maybe this is where my family is. I take a deep breath, my stomach flooding with butterflies. The smile on my face can't stretch far enough as I stand there and wait for someone to answer. But after a few minutes, nothing happens. No one answers the door. Strange. I knock again. Still nothing. Maybe they aren't home.

Giving up, I cross the street and try the next house. Again, no answer. The next house, same thing. And the next, nothing.

Are you fucking kidding me?

I did not come this far to just be left out here. I know someone has to be home. Who just leaves the lights on?

Pissed and frankly sick of this shit, I decide to peer into one of the windows. Well, I was right about one thing; there is someone home. Except inside are fucking *elves*. I'm in the goddamn north pole.

Inside, the elves are dressed in their stereotypical green outfits. The place is crowded with them, all moving quickly with purpose. One jumps up onto a wooden chair at a table to put the arms on a doll. Another screws the wheels onto a toy truck. All of them with a role to play, unable to steer away from their work.

Uh huh. *Alright.*

I knock on the window to get their attention. But they ignore me.

Fuck you too, I think.

Maybe if I look into a different window I'll have better luck. I go to the first house again to take a look. Okay, give me a second to look again because I don't believe it. Yes, alright, I'm seeing this right. Inside is none other than Santa Claus himself. Okay, *now* I've seen everything. His large red coat is hanging up on the wall with his boots placed underneath. He sits back on a recliner chair with his feet up on a stool. He's wearing his classic red pants with black suspenders over a white t-shirt. In his hand, he reads from a list so long the end is piled on the floor. He chuckles and takes a sip from his hot chocolate.

Again, I knock on the window and call out his name, but his eyes don't move from the list. What? Am I on the naughty list or something? Screw it, I say to myself and try the doorknob, but it doesn't budge. Maybe if I find the house Santa keeps his reindeer in, I can just ride one of them out of here.

What am I even saying? Elves? Santa Claus? Reindeer? And now that I think about it these houses look like they're made of gingerbread. This must be just some weird elaborate dream.

December 21st Day—it was in fact not a dream—**9.**

The singular detail that I woke up this morning in the snowbank of this village has told me that I am, indeed, awake. That's fucking *fantastic*. At least I'll have an interesting story to tell my family when I get out of here. I should try and get Santa's autograph for my daughter. Wait, do I have a daughter? I sit and try to picture what she looks like but nothing but the colour white comes to mind.

God, am I sick of the colour white.

"I just want to get out of here," I say to myself, slumping my body against the side of the house. Craning my neck to the sky, I watch as the snowflakes just keep falling.

"You can," a voice chirps.

I snap my neck back to see where the voice had come from. Across the street, almost camouflaged by the snow is an owl perched on the fence.

"Uh, did you just talk?" I ask. The bird turns its head around its body, its huge eyes blinking at me.

"I'll take your silence as a no." I must be going crazy. But then again, at least this owl in front of me is alive. A smile forms on my face as the loneliness I have felt disappears. It is nice to have company again even if I'm imagining a talking bird.

The owl hoots. "You must be pretty lonely out here, too. You're the only animal I've seen around here," I say.

"Way out," the bird says. I blink. Okay, this time I saw that bird speak. Its beak moved, and those words definitely came out of it.

"Way out?" I ask, my eyes widening. Does it mean a way out of this snow hell? Did the bird come from somewhere warm and snowless?

"Uh huh," The bird responds.

"Where? How?" I yell, disregarding how crazy I look talking to an owl.

It lifts a wing, pointing toward the houses and past where the stone path ends. In the distance, through the blizzard is what looks like a cave. A cave so large it stretches from the earth to the sky.

"Where does that lead to? How do I get there?" I ask, with excitement. But when I turn back to the owl, it's gone.

December 22nd Day 10

I've been pushing myself through this blizzard for a *whole* goddamn day and the cave seems just as far away. It's like the opposite of a sandstorm where you start to see mirages.

I'd prefer the hell out of sand than snow.

Every so often the earth seems to shake beneath me. It trembles briefly but causes the wind to pick up so strong it forces me to topple over. *Like I needed more challenges.*

Ten days. Ten days, and I haven't died of frostbite or starvation. I've seen elves, fucking *Santa Claus,* and even met a talking owl. I've concluded that I've just gone crazy. Or maybe this is the afterlife. Maybe I'm already dead.

December 23rd Day 11: I better be almost the fuck there.

This adventure wouldn't be so bad if something interesting happened. If I came across something a hell of a lot *cooler* than snow.

Okay, scratch that. Something warmer.

The cave still seems to be the exact same distance away that it did when I started heading towards it. If anything, it's just stretched higher to the sky.

A part of me misses that little village of elves. At least it was something different to look at than the colour white. I don't, however, miss how fucking lonely it felt to be completely ignored and left outside.

Just when I think I'll never see anything but snow ever again something moves in the corner of my eye. When I look I don't see anything at first. But then yes, there's something there. Something small and black in the distance. It looks like it's coming towards me. What even is it?

Crap. Run. Run. RUN!

A polar bear is racing its way towards me. Its body blends in with the snow, but its black snout and eyes are directed at me. When I said I wanted something interesting to happen, this is *not* what I had in mind. I thought maybe seeing a flower or two. Maybe even a Christmas tree. Not a goddamn polar bear.

So, frostbite and starvation didn't kill me, but this polar bear will. My legs can't seem to move fast enough through the heaps of snow. Dammit, if I could just reach the entrance to this cave I could hide and get away from this thing.

That's when at the most convenient time possible the earth shakes again. I fall face first into the snow. The polar bear? Oh well, *of course*, it isn't fazed by the fucking ground moving. It's still coming at me just as quickly. I fight through the snow, scrambling to my feet. The earth moves again just as I stand up. And down I go again. I peer over my shoulder. The polar bear is so close now there's no chance of escaping. I duck my head into the snow, covering my head with my hands like that'll help hide me.

The thud of its paws running towards me grows louder, almost as loud as the sound of my heart in my ears. In an instant, I feel the bear on top of me. Its paws pound against my body, but just as quickly, it's gone. I glance upward to see the polar bear has moved on, continuing its course towards the cave.

Strange, I don't feel any pain. Is it because my body is so numb from the cold? I try to stand and miraculously I am able to. Super strange. I feel shorter somehow but I'm still able to walk. So I continue my journey to the mysterious cave, this time hoping nothing interesting happens.

December 24th the **12th** day of Christmas.

I made it. I fucking did it.

The cave is, in fact, right in front of me. Looking up it appears to cover the whole sky. On the inside, I see a *giant* Christmas tree decorated with brightly coloured ornaments, the lights twinkling with presents placed underneath in gold and red paper. The faint sound of Christmas carols fill the cave. Stockings way too big for any feet I've seen, are hung up on the far wall. Other Christmas decorations of wreaths and mistletoe are hung around the cave. Lying at the front of the cave is a huge dog curled up as it naps. I can see an enormous brown sofa where a family sits in their Christmas themed pajamas. *My family?* There's a mom with her brown hair tied in a bun onto her head, handing cups of hot chocolate to a young boy and girl. The father sits, flicking channels on the massive T.V. across the room. On the television, I see a show about hikers traveling in snowy mountains. But most importantly, it looks fucking *warm* in there. They seem so happy. I wave to them to try and get their attention. But they don't acknowledge me. What's with everyone ignoring me? These people, as big as they are, are real. I know it. They have to be my family. I take a step forward hoping that if I enter the cave it will catch their attention. Except my body hits against a clear wall. How do I get in?

Wait, I see something else too. Ever so slightly I see the image of a snowman directly in front of me. But the image is see-through as if it's merely a reflection. The snowman looks rather silly missing his carrot nose and his hat pulled way too far down his forehead. The bottom of his face is completely covered by a scarf. I reach out to help the snowman. Maybe he's stuck between this glass wall, somewhere between this blizzard and the warm cave. But when I lift my arm to reach for him, his lifts too as if he can predict my movements. I try my other arm, and again his arm follows. Hold on...

December 25th Day, it doesn't fucking matter anymore.

Well, I figured it out. The big mystery. Merry fucking Christmas to me. I'm a goddamn snowman in a snow globe.

I pound against the wall in frustration, wanting to cry, wanting to scream. But nothing can change this. My life is hell.

Giving up I let my forehead rest against the glass wall looking longingly at the family on the other side. They're laughing and hugging each other without a care in the world. I catch myself forming a smile on my face. Sure, I can't be right beside them. But yes, they are my family. I get to see how happy they are. I get to enjoy Christmas right along with them. I have the upmost perfect view and I wouldn't change it for all the warmth in the world.

That's when the little boy hops down from the couch and comes running to me. The grin stretched across his face warms my heart.

Yes. This is what true warmth feels like.

The boy shakes the globe, the snowstorm picking up stronger with each shake. I lose my balance and I too am flying through the air.

December 13th Day One….

Sam Baker

—is horrified of boring people with her ridiculously average life, so she creates fictional worlds to live vicariously through them. She is usually over-obsessing about her next story or researching new ways to fictionally maim someone. Her other hobbies include impersonating a sloth, preparing for the apocalypse, and daydreaming about hypothetical situations that will never actually happen. Although her genres aren't limited, she currently writes science fiction. Look for her novel *Variant Wars* to read more of her work.

J Douglas Burton

—is an American who grew up in Scotland - but don't hold either one of those against him. He's a nice enough guy, really. He is the writer of, among other things, the YA fantasy series "The Sleepwar Saga".

Brittany Evans

—is an awkward hermit from the middle of nowhere in Ontario, Canada. She prefers writing Fantasy, but will often dip her toes in her Contemporary. She is a helpless romantic that can't help but include some form of romance in her stories. When not writing she can be found drowning in her TBR pile.

Krystle Kwiatkowski

—is a screenwriter from Georgia. She specializes in stories pertaining to the supernatural and aims to create her own TV show. While film is her priority, she plots to publish novels in the future. She loves writing in her Hobbit Hole when she's not on her throne in Hell.

Chelsea Lauren

— is a New York native now living in Florida. When she isn't basking in the sunshine and walking the beach (talking to her characters), she can be found polishing her skills as a workaholic. But don't worry, she balances the stress with her friends, Mickey and Minnie. In between extremes, you'll find her drinking an immense amount of coffee. Her debut novel *Underneath the Whiskey* was released May 2017!

Paul E. Petty

—is a Young Adult author from the small town of Ore City, Texas. He is a Grammar Nazi and has a habit of buying books faster than he can read them. When not writing or being a responsible adult, he can usually be found wasting time on Twitter. He currently resides in Gilmer, Texas.

Acknowledgements

Thank you to each and every person who has supported us. Without you, none of us would have made it this far, nor would we have ever met each other. So, thank you for everything you've done.

—the Winter Neverlanders